DEDICATION

For those that give everything for freedom.

ACKNOWLEDGMENTS

Even an introvert like me can't do it all by herself. First, I'd like to thank all those that believed in me, provided me feedback, criticism and support- Jared and all the beta readers. Thanks to my husband, my boyfriend, my adventure partner, my everything- for working hard to give me the opportunity to chase my dreams. I'd like to thank my mom, for being the most awesome mom on the planet- she always told me I could do whatever I set my mind to- this book proves that's true.

PART I

Bum Fuck Egypt

1

Ryan

Contrary to what a lot of people think, I never intended on becoming the first female Navy Seal. It was politics that had gotten me into the program, but it was my own sheer drive, help from a bad-ass trainer (former Delta force), and determination that had me graduating BUD/S training. It was again politics that had me flying out of Coronado, California to Virginia to be placed with a team on a test run basis a few weeks after graduation. Sure, my father is Vice Admiral Richard Ryan.

A veteran SEAL himself, who passed the traits of fortitude, discipline, and sheer stubbornness onto me, his baby daughter. His intentions were for me to grow up and be an independent strong woman. Not that I would grow up and put my skills to use in dangerous situations. But I had used my favorite-child status with him to get what I wanted -field experience.

The deal we struck was that if he convinced SOCOM to put me on a team that was actively deployed, then I would retire after three years with the unspoken: settle down and get married tag line. I also agreed that should I ever be injured in the line of duty – no matter how minor - I would go into 'early retirement.'

Standing at attention outside the Captain's office, I watched the coming and goings of the administrative staff, shuffling papers, drinking coffee, tapping away at their computers, and generally paying me no mind. Sure, I get the occasional look as a woman in 'teagues usually gets among officers. I was here to meet my new commanding officer and be directed to THE team. MY team.

I am unaccountably nervous- and tapping my index finger on the back of my hand behind my back – the only outward sign of my inner emotions. I breathe deep and clear my mind. I had only been waiting about fifteen minutes, but the power play rankled.

Suddenly the door to my right whooshes open and Captain Mendoza steps out to acknowledge me. We do the required salutes.

"Ryan! At ease," are his first words to me.

He reaches out and shakes my hand. Second power play of the day is him squeezing so hard I am sure the bones in my hand grind against each other. Hardly the first time this has happened. I just roll with it, giving back as good as I get while he takes my measure. He is an affable looking military man, crinkles at his eyes, short gray hair, intelligent eyes that seem a bit tired, but not uncalculating.

He holds his office door open for me, in a gesture of come on in.

As we enter, he speaks, "Come in, Ryan. Meet Chief Broussard and take a seat."

The form in question, Chief Broussard, is planted against the front of the desk. Tall, wide-shouldered man, lean, but with a proportionate musculature. His face sporting three days worth of dark stubble. Chestnut, mussed hair and calculating eyes. Eyes that narrow with annoyance at me, as he crosses his arms in front of his chest after the required salutes.

He lets his gaze roam from the top of my head to the bottom of my feet. And back up again.

I feel heat warm my cheeks and neck.
The silence and his perusal are abruptly shattered by his quietly explosive, "FUCK NO!"

Turning to the captain he slams both his hands palm down on the desk and leans over to stress his refusal to the Captain; I take the chance to give him the same one over he had just given me. Broad shoulders, lean waist, and taut butt. Yep, he is good looking and has a fit body. So does just about every other SEAL I had been in contact with...and they all carry the same egotistical chip on their shoulders.

Broussard starts, "She's not on my team. She just fucking blushed!"

Captain Mendoza turns his gaze from the computer in front of him to Broussard, then to me.

He looks at me from over the top of his bifocals. "Sit down, Ryan. Broussard, calm down. It's a trial basis. And we all know..." He looks back at me.

I sit calmly in the chair even though his words are burning like acid in my gut.

He had been going to say, we all know she is going to fail or the Navy won't really put her in action.
Broussard growls. There's no other word for the grunt that rolls from his throat. He raps his knuckles on top of the desk before turning to face me again. We lock eyes.

"Sir, " he began, "this is," he pauses without looking away, "...unacceptable."

We are now locked into an unofficial staring contest. No way am I looking away. His eyes are hazel, caramel center surrounded by a mossy green framed by dark brown lashes. Too beautiful to be glaring at me in such a way.

"These are direct orders down from SOCOM. I know the situation is not ideal, but let's just give it some time and see what happens," comes the captain's voice from behind Broussard.

Out the corner of my eye, I see the captain rise from his desk and step around. He walks just to the other side of Broussard and then steps between us while handing Broussard a folder.

The staring contest is broken. A tie. I should be grateful to Captain Mendoza for breaking it up. Any longer and I might have caved. Chief Broussard's gaze is intimidating to say the least. I felt as though he had been reading every mistake I'd ever made in my eyes, seeing every shortcoming on my face. Disconcerting to say the least.

"You have your orders, Broussard. I expect to be kept up to date."

The captain walks back around the desk, sits in his chair, and starts typing on his computer.

"You're both dismissed."

Following Chief Broussard out of the office building and into the afternoon sunlight, I wait for his next command.

"C'mon. We have a team briefing in thirty minutes. Then afternoon PT."

I just nod and follow him to a black jeep in the parking lot.

"Get in."

A short and silent ride ensues. I take in all the details of him, his car, the base. He wears a wedding band. His car smells like a fancy air freshener, clean and piney. Not much else. The base is nondescript, brown or gray buildings, newly paved roads, blue sky.

Parking in front of one of the many concrete gray nondescript buildings, Broussard grabs the folder he had put on his dash and proceeds to exit the jeep without a word. He pauses at the metal entrance door of the building.

He holds it open for me, but his whole demeanor is annoyance- not polite. So the gesture of kindness is lost on me. As I go through, I give my eyes a moment to adjust to the dimly lit interior.

A conference table directly ahead, surrounded by four of five scarred metal desks. Light from fluorescents and a few skylights. There are two men sitting at those desks that look up when we enter.

"Hey Chief Broussy! I thought new recruits were coming in next week!"

Before I can introduce myself, 'Broussy' cut in with, "Ryan. A word in my office."

He turns a sharp right down a small hallway off to the side.

Chief Broussard has the corner office. But it is nondescript and plain - nothing like the military to humble you. Crappy furniture- a wood laminate topped desk pockmarked with coffee cup circles, in front of two metal folding chairs. A scarred brown leather couch sits lumpy and dejected against one wall. Behind the desk is another man, blond hair and blue eyes that looks up as we enter.

Broussard slides the folder he was holding onto the desk and then perches on one corner of it with his arms crossed, staring me down again. No introductions then.

"OK. How many dicks did you suck to get here?"

I curls one side of my lip up on an exhale breath and cross my arms over my own chest in mimic of him.
I start with, "Really? How original! A navy guy with a chauvinistic attitude."

I see his jaw tense. Maybe honey catches more flies than vinegar, but I've never been one to stand down from such a challenge.

"It's really, SIR?"
"Sir."

"Sit down and listen up, Ryan."

"I prefer to stand...sir."

"Fine. You're on MY team now. And I don't put up with bitch attitudes, whining, or falling behind. You don't carry your weight? You're out. You bitch about the sand in your fucking Prada shoe? You're out! You do anything at any time I don't like? You're out. I don't give two fucks who your daddy is."

He finishes his tirade. There really is no argument from me. Sounds like a plan I am already on board with. I couldn't and wouldn't expect less from anyone else on the team. I place my hands behind my back in parade rest and gave him a nod, "Yes Sir."

More staring at me, getting my measure.

He closes his eyes and pinches the bridge of his nose with his thumb and forefinger in a gesture of tiredness and resignation.

"FUCK." He sighs breathes out heavily in resignation, "Reed, this is Ryan, the newest member of SEAL Team Four."

And that is my introduction to the team.

2

I am a fuckin' pariah. Running my hands through my
short brown choppy hair- I make it stick up in odd angles
while giving myself a critical once over in the mirror. Gray
eyes, little button nose, as my older sister describes it, and
lips a tad too full to be decent and currently pulled into a
frown.

Four months. Four fucking months of sitting on the
sidelines and watching the team deploy and complete
missions.

Maybe this is how I will spend my time with the SEALs.
What a fucking waste.

I sigh and turn from the mirror. Not even the
endorphins from PT are cheering me up like they normally
do. I hate that I am a middle packer in the runs, but to be
honest the legs that stand me tall at 5'10 are probably the
only physical advantage I possess...and even with that I am
just enough to be mediocre.

It's a good thing I trained with a professional in the time
between the Marines and the Navy, or else I would have
never made it through BUD/S. There is a debriefing in
thirty minutes so I hurriedly slip into my serviceable black
cotton underwear and two sports bras. I do a jump, looking
at my boobs just to make sure there is no unnecessary or

extra jiggling. Two bra approved. I'm a sexless soldier - or as sexless as I can get with smashed breasts.

Gray t-shirt and digital camo pants complete my uniform.

As I dress, I delve a little deeper into my melancholy. This might be the first time since I've left home that I've been homesick. I am a part of the team by proximity only really. Always, I'm assigned as the liaison (communicator between command and the team) while they are on missions. Usually, this position rotates, but since I've been on the team- it's always me.

I sit down on the bed and pull on my boots.

Petty officer Gonzalez opens the door and comes into our shared space.

"Hey Ryan! How goes it?"

Petty Officer Gonzalez is a medic in the Corps. We share a room in the barracks.

I finish tying and grimace at her.

At my look, she gives me a, "I hear ya!" Followed by a half-hearted "Hoo-yah," as she flops on her bed.

She is a middle child in a horde of thirteen. I think her mother was an original immigrant from Mexico, and PO Gonzalez had enlisted to try and get somewhere, anywhere, in life besides behind a cleaning cart.

She is about five years younger than me, but we gel as best we can being two complete strangers with very little in common besides our anatomy. I leave her with a short 'See ya later."

I jog the mile to the offices of seal team four. Arriving an hour early than what's needed, but this is necessity after one particular instance when I was fifteen minutes late after arriving thirty minutes early – just one of the guys hazing rituals.

I take my post at one of the desks in the corner and twirl a pen around while doodling on a notepad.

The office is quiet. Just the hum of the air conditioner

THE DISTANCE BETWEEN DREAMS

and computers. Soon, the whirring blades of a helicopter reach my ears, the whoop whoops getting louder and louder until the noise is near deafening as it lands just out the backside of our office.

The team filters in, dirty and sweaty, looking tired and smelling ripe. Five days in the field really brings out their man-smell.

T-Rex takes the seat next to me with a curt nod. He is a good guy. From Texas, he has a wife and kid that he lives with in a townhouse off base- he and Reed are about the only two that acknowledge my presence on a regular basis. He hooks his thumbs at the shoulders of his Kevlar vest and leans back in a semi-relaxed position next to me.

Chief Broussard comes in next to last, and his eyes scan the room until they come to a stop on me. Our gaze holds one heartbeat. Two. My heart rate accelerates. *I am not attracted to him, I am not attracted to him, I am not attracted to him.* This mantra I repeat over and over in my head. I mean I am surrounded by a plethora of fine male specimens. I will not crush on my commander. His hazel eyes finally move past me and keep roving as he pulls off his helmet and places it on the conference table.

The barrel of his .308 is sticking up over his left shoulder, while his AR is strapped across his front. I ignore the fluttering in my belly at the strong masculine image he projects.

"Alright Pussies!" He raps the tabletop with his knuckles.

A cheer of "Broussy's Pussies!" goes up; followed by "Hoo-Yah!"

This cheer is a direct association with myself- they started employing it just two weeks after I came on the team.

"Target neutralized. Goods secure. As always...security code Tango Sierra fifty-two. Tango Sierra. Any questions? No. Good? PT resumes in 4 days. Enjoy your holidays, ladies."

The four day hiatus was Thanksgiving break.

"RYAN!"

I turn my gaze from where I was watching the rest of the team filter out the door.

"Yes sir?"

"You got any reports? Got the debriefing report for me to sign?"

I reach back to the desk behind me and grab the report I had typed up six hours ago from the desk.

"Right here sir."

I grab a pen from the desk and take both the report and pen to him where he is still standing at the table.

He runs a hand through his hair while his eyes remain fixed on the papers.

"You going to see family tomorrow, Ryan?"

His personal question takes me aback for a moment.

He lifts his gaze from the paper to look at me.

"No sir."

He looks back at the paper and I see his eyes sweeping back and forth as he reads the text. His brow is drawn in concentration.

"Why not?"

This conversation has gotten intensely personally in a short matter of time.

I shift on my feet.

"Um, you know…just uh…" I rub the back of my neck trying to think of something to say.

I hadn't been home for THE holidays in 3 years. You know, Thanksgiving OR Christmas. It is a sore spot between my father and I. But really, with two older sisters getting married and popping out kids left and right, every trip home feels like a noose tightening around my throat. And I can't stand it.

Chief Broussard lays the papers down on the desk and places his palm down beside them as he reaches for the pen.

"You know, Ryan, family is a terrible thing to waste."

He signs the paper with a flourish and disappears out the door.

His words hang in the air. Of course he probably knows my family. My father, the top Navy Admiral. My sisters, married to beautiful, strong military men with cute adorbs babies. Fuck that shit. They all are a direct threat to my freedom and independence. I resent that Chief Broussard has brought them up. I had planned a fantastic Thanksgiving- living it up on junk food and sleeping in a carb and sugar induced coma-like state. Now, thanks to he-who-shall-not-be-noticed, I have guilt weighing my shoulders down.

I snap up the signed papers and quickly scan them in at the computer terminal. I send them off to our XO and then began looking at plane tickets. It might cost me a fortune, but I am pretty sure I can catch the red eye out of DC to LA and then rent a car for the drive to Oceanside where dad lives.

3

After my flight lands and I get a rental car, I stop at a convenience store to get a Red Bull. Coffee is just not going to do it after the little bit of sleep I had gotten on the flight. I'm a light sleeper- and a plane full of holiday travellers had me too ill at ease to be able to relax.

I pull out my cell phone and find the contact "Dad house." I hit the call button and feel a strange nervousness in my stomach as I listened to the tinny ring in my ear.

After three rings a guttural, "Hello, Everly," sounds over the line. I recognize the voice of my brother–in-law, Sean.

"Sean. Hey."

"Hey yourself. Didn't expect to hear from you today after your dad told us you couldn't make it in this year again."

I look out over the nearly empty parking lot of the convenience store and tap the top of the steering wheel. I can hear the TV on in the background.

"Sean, is Dad there?"

"Yea, he's here. Drinking his coffee. Hold on."

I hear muffled sounds. Sean covering the receiver with the palm of his hand.

"Rick, it's Everly," can still be heard as Sean hands the phone to my dad- letting him know who's on the other end. My dad's voice on the line, "Everly, what is it? Everything ok?"

I chuckle a bit. I guess an unexpected phone call warrants some worry.

"I'm fine, Dad. Just about an hour out of Oceanside. Need me to pick up any last minute groceries on my way in?"

"You're in Cali? "

"Yea, I uh...got leave last minute."

"Well c'mon; We got the turkey in the oven, and you need to get here before your sister tries to make that awful southern dressing this year instead of traditional stuffing. I don't care if Sean is from Georgia, she put way too much salt in it last year."

I smile at that. "Yea, Dad. Im'ma be there in an hour."

"Good, cause I need some good 'ole fashioned Ryan reinforcements. God knows, I love your sisters and their broods, but sheesh, the only Ryan among them is Liberty."

Liberty is the oldest of my four nieces and nephews. I was introduced to her on her first birthday, July 4th, five years ago, just before I discharged from the Marines. Her wiggling little body and chubby pink face with ineffectual flailing fists was enough to scare me into swearing that I would never have kids. I mean, I guess she was cute, but she was just so dang needy. I was happy to hand her back to my sister when her tiny face scrunched up and she began some pathetic whimpering.

"Ok Dad. Hold down the fort. I'm coming."

We disconnect and I put the car in gear. I take a deep breath and maneuvered out of the parking lot. Yea. Family.

Pulling into my dad's driveway, I shut off the rental and take another fortifying breath. The family situation is only stressful on my side. Had been since David's death eight years ago when I made the decision to take his place serving my country in the military. It always hits home how much differently my life could have been had he lived. Had we gotten married and decided to move forward with the American dream; two kids, mortgage and mini-van. Just like my sisters, who can't understand why after sacrificing a true love at such a young age, I would then sacrifice my life in his name in the military.

I can't explain it to them. I can't explain that I would never be just another survivor. I would be the fighter. I will never stand to be on the sidelines. I will be the one to throw the punches and direct the path of my life. Action instead of reaction.

I sigh and grab my bag from the passenger seat.

Pushing open the car door, I walk the path to the front door and had a moment of awkwardness on whether or not I should just walk on in or ring the doorbell.

Before a decision can be made, the door swings inward and my sister's annoyed visage appears, her hair flying back from her flushed face in the force of displaced air from her volatile opening of the door.

On her hip a fat little cherub baby is crying and red-faced.

"EVERLY. Get your ass in here!"

The heat in her words is softened by the smile curling her lips and the twinkle in her eyes that looks suspiciously like tears forming.

Stepping over the threshold she half hugs me with the arm that isn't wrapped around her child. This brings my face in direct line with baby exhibit A as I leaned down to return her embrace. Both my sisters are a bit shorter than me, I was the lucky one to inherit dad's tall genes. The baby and I survey each other with curious eyes.

I take a step back and look over the newest member of the family that I have yet to meet. Reaching my hand out, I give Baby A a little tickle and goochie-goochie-goo on his cheek, as this is the sole right of Aunties, like myself.

But my sister has other plans and is too quick for me.

"Here, take him. I've got to check on things in the kitchen."

Before I can protest, she has Baby A thrust out in a weird offering I don't want to take, but feel compelled to do since his mom seems to be abandoning him to my care. Sneaky bitch. At least he has stopped crying and is just looking at me curiously as I struggle to balance him on my left hip and my bag on my right shoulder. The struggle is real. He's a fat little turd.

"Geez, Kinsey, what are you feeding him? He weighs like twenty pounds."

She has stepped back away from us and clasps her hands underneath her chin. The tears are real now, and she is smiling a weird wavering smile and crying at the same time.

"I'm so happy to see you!"

She gives me another half hug and we repeat the precarious dance we did before in reverse.

"And little Sean just loves you!"

Right, this is little Sean. I probably should make sure I don't want to Freudian slip and call him 'baby exhibit A' when I reference him.

She turns and makes a break down the hall to the kitchen.

I slide my bag off my shoulder and let it fall to the floor. I go to follow my sister and find a safe place to deposit this baby. He now seems to have some drool coming out of his mouth, and it's making a wet spot on my leather jacket.

Before I can pass the living room on the way to the kitchen though, I am waylaid again, this time by a little terrorist known as my niece, Liberty. She comes running and screaming out of the living room and wraps her arms around my legs in an effective stopping maneuver.

"AUNTIE EVERLY! AUNTIE EVERLY! AUNTIE EVERLY!"

Her father and my brother-in-law, Brent, is right behind her though, and quickly scoops her up while I awkwardly pat her back.

"Liberty Bell, give her some room. Hey Everly."

He gives me a one armed hug and kisses my forehead.

"So good to see you."

I repeat the same back to him. Then the flood of hugs and greetings really commences. My father, Admiral Rick, my sister Isabelle (married to Brent) and my other brother in law, Sean bring on the hug receiving line. Then while Izzy finally takes little Sean from my arms, I get to give a proper hug to Liberty, Trevor, and little baby Emma, almost the same age as little Sean.

My sisters are two sides of the same coin. From their physical appearances, dark hair, dark eyes (like my mother) to their nurturing personalities and even their life timelines-getting married and popping out kids in tandem almost. Liberty was the oldest at five, then Trevor at three and a half, followed by Emma at a year, and finally little Sean at eight months.

A distinct fart noise comes from the vicinity of little Sean's diaper.

"Eww gross." This from Liberty who knows exactly what such a noise means. My dad claps his hands once.

"All right, let's break this up and give Everly some breathing room."

Everyone disperses from the living room as dad puts his arms around my shoulder and hugs me again.

"So good to have you home, Everly."

It's good to be home. Even when home stresses you out and puts your heart and emotions in blender on high speed.

4

I settle into my seat on the plane and wait for the rest of the passengers to board even though there weren't that many. My 1900 flight out of San Fran had one layover in Atlanta where I switched planes. I'd be arriving at four in the morning on Sunday. My day to catch up on some Z's and fold some laundry. I lean back against the headrest and shut my eyes while the handful of other passengers shuffle down the aisle and take their seats.

Thankfully, because this is an airline that doesn't assign seats, and a late night connection, I was able to get a prime window seat and the peace that comes with not being bumped every ten seconds on an aisle seat.

A presence stops at my row. I slant my eyes open and see a man placing his bag in the overhead compartment above my seat. His shirt rides up a little to reveal the tiniest sliver of muscled flesh and a deliciously tiny happy trail that disappears into the waistband of his jeans. It's been too long if I am salivating over this barest glimpse of a stranger.

I raise my eyes to his chest; it is impressively broad, clothed in a scrumptious faded green Henley. I close my eyes shut and turn my head forward hastily before he catches me staring. His weight drops in the aisle seat of my row and his scent wafts my way. Warm, clean masculine scent. I half smile to myself and feel a warm blush come into my cheeks as I imagine grabbing whoever this stranger is and having my way with him.

"Hey, Ryan."

My eyes pop open. Mr. Aisle seat with the very happy trail is none other than Senior Chief Eric Broussard. My CO.

SHIT. FUCK. SHIT. FUCK.

"Cat got your tongue?"

He half smiles at me as he leans over the armrest, his shoulder leaning in my direction. Bringing with it his delectable scent in a warm cloud of masculinity.

"Chief Broussard."

This is the sum total of my eloquent and loquacious dialogue. My brain is too busy trying to process that the object of my momentary desire is none other than my CO. And that now he is sitting next to me for the next hour and half.

His hazel eyes are piercing into mine, but there is this definite crinkle at the corner of his, his half smile still in place.

"How was your family, Ryan?"

I take a deep breath and look down at my lap.

"Very good, sir."

One flight attendant closes the exterior doors and another begins demonstrating the necessary pre-flight safety spiel. I pretend to listen while ignoring the strained awkwardness in the space between myself and the man one seat away from me.

As the plane begins its taxi to the runway, Broussard leans back in his seat and stretches his legs out in front of him. Seemingly dismissing me.

I take a deep breath. Maybe the flight won't be so bad if we can just ignore each other.

I drum my fingers on the armrest. Just as we reach altitude, Broussard turns towards me again.

"So what exactly is your story, Ryan?"

He's not really smiling anymore. His brow is creased in a question. Whether he really cares or not I can't guess.

Should I trust him? He is my commander, I know should I win myself into his graces, things would be smoother between me and the team. No. I shake my head. I've had too many run-ins with egotistical macho men. Men who think the only place for a woman is in the kitchen. Maybe not literally...but I know his type.

"I have no story...sir."

It comes out snarky even though I didn't mean it to have an edge. Guess my inner hate fire just slipped out. His facial expression changes into command mode. Straight set lips, slightly clenched jaw, flat eyes.

I flash back to my teenage rebel years when my father used to do the same thing to me after I had done something or said something that was a reflection of my 'bad attitude.'

An answering rebellious energy unfurls in my belly. I clench my fist and look away from him out the window.

I hear him shift in his seat.

"No story, huh? Just a cutthroat G.I. fucking Jane?"

I don't look away from the window. His words are nothing I haven't heard a thousand times over.

"I'll give you props, Ryan. Every test you've taken so far, you've passed. But real life is not a test. There are lives depending on you. Not just mine. And not just your team's."

I focus my eyes away from the outside blackness and on his face reflection. His whole body is leaning over the middle seat. Arms crossed on the armrest. His face is serious. The low light of the cabin and the hum of the engines have created a reluctant intimacy- we are in our own pocket of space, never this close before and probably never this close again.

"Every life you give or take is a rock thrown into a pond. The ripples of that life resonate out and crash against each other. There's repercussions that you just don't fucking understand."

I let his words wash over me. I turn back to face him. I unabashedly stare into his eyes. At his impossibly long eyelashes narrowed in disdain. His eyes are sharp, scrutinizing and captivating..

"That's where you are mistaken, sir. I do understand."

I turn forward and reach under my seat pulling out my iPod from my messenger bag at my feet. I plug the ear buds into my ears and turn on some *Florence + The Machine*.

My annoyance is trolling in my gut. Every man I've ever come into contact with in the military has had a chip on their shoulder about a woman in their workplace. Some are openly against it. Some passively aggressive. I've brushed it off a million times. It hadn't fucking mattered. I've proven myself again and again. I can do it. Not because I am an uber-feminist, a lesbian, a man-hater, or just a stone cold bitch.

I can do it and am doing it because I made a fucking promise.

And it fucking mattered.

5

Broussard

I watch her plug in her ear buds and turn away from me a last time.

FUCK. I hate it when women play the silent game.

There was nothing that annoyed me more or quickly crippled my resolve.

I sigh. Thank god this is a short flight.

Pushing the seatback to recline, I study Ryan in my peripheral vision. Her short hair in wild disarray. I don't even know if this artfully created or just messily happenstance.

Her long legs (I know they are long because she is five-ten according to her file- but I'd seen them in shorts too) are encased in worn jeans, maybe dark once, but now an indigo blue, with white-worn seams. Gray t-shirt and black scarf. Her breasts rise and fall with her measured breaths. Shit! Should I even be noticing her breasts? I hastily adjust my line of sight. Her feet are in worn cross trainers. The bag at her feet, simple black fabric, nothing different about it.... except a Boston Red Sox cap clipped around the strap.

This is curious. A safer topic than her breasts for me to puzzle over. Her father, the Admiral, is based in

21

California. I rack my brain trying to remember if he is originally from Boston. I don't think so. Her mom? No. Shit. It is her boyfriend. She has a boyfriend.

I let the conclusion wash over me. At first I am in disbelief. She is so stubbornly independent, and cantankerous, who would date her?

I would. The realization hits me with the same effect of a nuclear bomb going off.

I would date her. I am attracted to Ryan. Everly Ryan. I take another eyeball liberty over her.

No. I am not. She's a subordinate. Just another one of my team. I feel responsible for her life. A life that is tenfold more difficult to protect as part of my team just from the sole fact that she is a SHE.

That's what I've been feeling. Protective.

I breath deep, and exhale a sigh of relief. Yes. Protective. This makes much more sense than jealousy and attraction.

I sneak another glance at her. She has her eyes closed. Head leaned against the window. She's softer this way. Almost vulnerable.

She seems a thousand years younger than me. I do the mental calculations in my head. I'm thirty-three. She's twenty-seven. Six years. Luke's almost six. She could've given birth to Luke....

The idea flies into my head with disturbing ramifications. My thoughts are now churning a hundred miles a minute.

She could be a mother. But she is a soldier. She would've been twenty-two when Luke was born. She had been in boot camp for the Marines if I remember correctly from her file...when I was at Luke's birth with my then wife, Miranda. I clearly see a picture of Miranda in my mind's eye, swollen with Luke as she met me at the airport when I was returning from a deployment. Only Miranda's face of ecstatic joy begins to blur, turning into the face of Everly Ryan with bad attitude and sexy full lips.

A dinging interrupts my daydream.

"Please return your seats to the upright position. Our captain has just informed me we are making our final descent into Norfolk Regional. The time is 4:36 AM Eastern time, our conditions are favorable."

6

Ryan

The next day's four-thirty AM comes with a massive headache. Shit. It was like I drank half a bottle of tequila last night. Rolling off my bunk, I slip on the socks and running shoes that I keep right next to the bed. I always sleep in my running clothes. Not because it's extra motivating or cuts down on my getting ready time...I just am a really hard sleeper when I feel safe and it takes a good thirty minutes for my brain to start to function after I am "awake."

A quick swipe of tooth paste across my teeth, and some combination moisturizer sunscreen on my face and I am ready to go.

As I jog down the stairs of the barracks, my stomach feels even rockier. My body feels tired. Ugh, this will make the next 13 miles fantastic. Must be an emotional hangover from the holiday weekend. Usually I do a warm up by jogging to the long way round to the rendezvous point, but today, it feels like too much work, so instead I take the shortcut between buildings to get to our office parking lot.

Some of the team is already there doing stretches and they gave me nods of hello in the predawn darkness.

I reach down and touch my toes. My vision swims. I lean up quickly. I start to sweat, even though it is only about forty or so degrees out.

The rest of the team shows up, some in their vehicles, some on foot.

Broussard, I noticed, had come in his jeep; he does a silent and quick head count, then he is off. The rest of us fall in behind him.

I am middle of the pack like I usually am for the first four miles. My headache is pounding in time with my feet on the pavement. When Broussard leads the group off the pavement and through a hiking path that would take us through the woods then to the beach before we make a return loop, I feel that strange pooling of saliva in my mouth that is a precursor for vomiting. I fall behind Reed and tamp the feeling down.

I will not puke. I will not puke. I will NOT puke.

I chant it over and over in my head in disbelief. I hadn't even made it seven miles and am back of the pack; T-Rex just passed me for crissakes and he is always last of the group. I have never been last before. That shameful feeling spurs me on, even though the sweat on my forehead is clammy and my insides are shaky. FUCK. Is this run over yet?

I don't know how I make it the last five miles. My legs are noodles and I know, I know the minute I stop I will be done-zo.

As soon as my feet cross the pavement into the parking lot, Broussard's yell carries over to me.

"RYAN! Your ass-over here now!"

A few of the team are still in the lot, doing cool down stretches, pushups etc.

I jog over to Broussard and come to parade rest. My stomach...is not ok.

25

"WHAT THE FUCK, RYAN? ARE YOU ON YOUR PERIOD?"

Ok, I knew I was last of the pack, and that would get me some ribbing. It's the first time I had slipped up and given him something to pounce on. But sheesh, to have my ovaries become part of the conversation so fast really irks me. Something bad happens then. I had stopped. My stomach betrays me. And it is a violent betrayal. The projectile vomit that comes up is mostly bile and water. I am fast enough to turn to my right, instead of throwing up all over Broussard. But as I watch the water-bile mix hit the pavement, I can only close my eyes in relief that my stomach muscles are no longer coming up through my throat.

This is bad. I just threw up in front of my team. I take a deep breath in my bent over position and slowly straighten back into parade rest, wiping the back of my hand across my mouth. At least my stomach feels a bit better. I can't directly meet Broussard's eyes, I look over his shoulder instead.

"FUCK. Clean this up and get out of my sight, Ryan!"

He turns and slams the door into the office after himself. The few other guys in the lot have a mix of awe, disgust and hilarity on their faces.

Peppers is the first one to break the silence.

"Holy shit, Ryan! You just puked all over the CO!"

This sets Reed and Brody off into peals of laughter. I give them the finger and go inside to the break room to get a pitcher of water to rinse the vomit off the pavement. I splash some on my face while I'm at it.

I am really just relieved that Broussard hadn't made me do push-ups into the vomit. Yea, I'd seen that once at basic. I am feeling really shaky. So, once I had rinsed the pavement, I grab a Gatorade from the little fridge and chug it. Bad move.

I rush into the locker room and throw it all up in Technicolor neon green into the sink. I rest my forehead on the cool porcelain of the sink.

I ponder my symptoms. It is either a stomach bug or the flu. If it is the flu, I'd be miserable for a few more days. I could try to soldier on or I could ask Gonzalez if she had some Tamiflu she could give me. Thinking about being last on the run today had me making up my mind. I ease out the front door without running into anyone and take the shortcut back to my barracks. Luckily enough Gonzalez is there putting on her shoes getting ready to leave for work.

"Hey, Ryan. Don't usually see you around this early."

Full body shivers take over as I say, "Listen, Gonzalez. I need that stuff, the Tamiflu."

She looks me over.

"You think you got the flu? Here sit down. What are your symptoms?"

I sit on my foot locker.

"Fever, vomiting, headache and general feeling of overall shittiness."

She pulls her lanyard with her credentials over her head.

"You do look a little green around the gills. C'mon I'll give you a ride to the clinic. We can test to see if you have the flu for sure. Plus, Dr. Z can send over an excuse to your XO so you can get a free pass for a few days to rest up."

I nod my agreement. Rest probably couldn't hurt. Plus I am no hurry to see Broussard after that puke-fest.

One test later, it is confirmed I have the flu. The doctor gives me the Tamiflu shot, and a prescription for plenty of rest and drinking plenty of liquids.

I walk back to the barracks- I am too proud to ask Gonzalez for a ride back from the clinic, plus it's only about three miles. It isn't even eleven yet. But I hit the mattress and pull the blanket over my body the second I get to my bunk. It feels phenomenal to be horizontal. That is my last thought before I sleep through the day and half the night. I wake up at 1500 with a growling stomach. I make a slice of toast with Gonzalez's little toaster, eat it and promptly go back to sleep.

7

I am back at my routine by Thursday. The guys give me a good bit of ribbing, and let me know three other people have come down with the flu- including the CO, Broussard. Reed leads the PT that morning, and I am happy to get my middle of pack placement back. Once we were all back and showered and in the conference room for our 0900 briefing, the fun banter begins.

"Good thing that wasn't morning sickness, Ryan. Hate to have caught a pregnancy!" This from Peppers, apparently our team comedian.

I don't have a come back for him besides, "Fuck off, dickhead."

Creative insult, I know.

I take a seat and wait for what else might come out of these asshole's mouths. I love them and hate them. Good-natured jerking around is and always will be part of the team building. I understand the psychology of it, but so far they had really left off giving me too hard a time.

"So Princess Pukey, who are you gonna barf on today?"

This from Daniels, he is the other newbie that came on the team at the same time I did.

"If you're lucky, Daniels, it might be you."

I smile my best evil smile at him. Guffaws and "oohs" erupt.

Seriously, these guys are worse than high-schoolers.

Thankfully, Reed comes in then and the shit talking dies down.

I listen as he briefs us on the next week's training mission. But my brain is replaying the pissed off look on Broussard's face when I had thrown up right at his feet.

An hour or so later, we were dismissed for "brunch." It is really just an early and long lunch break, before we have to be on the range in the early afternoon.

As the guys began to filter out, I stand and pick up my notepad.

"Hey Ryan," from Reed, "You're D.D. tomorrow night. I'll pick the van up; just meet us here at twenty hundred sharp."

Looks like the puke episode has actually broken the ice with the team. Go figure.

About once a month the mostly single members of the team pile into a rented van and go out on the town to satisfy their entertainment needs by drinking and picking up women, etc. While being their chauffeur is hardly high entertainment for me, I do recognize it for what it was- an invitation to be part of the team.

"Yes sir. Twenty hundred sharp."

8

I am fifteen minutes early. The van is already parked in the lot. So is Reed's truck. I pull open the door to the office and let it close behind me.

The office is quiet. Reed is in the conference room, feet propped up on the table, chair tipped back and tossing something back and forth in his hands.

"Ryan!" he says when he sees me enter.

"Sir."

He slams his feet down on the floor. He is wearing civvies- jeans and a nice button down shirt. I too am wearing jeans, but I had thrown my favorite caramel leather jacket on over my black t-shirt. My black scarf and cross trainers complete the outfit. And oh yea. I had put on mascara. It was the only concession to makeup I think I could make without risking them tearing me to pieces over it.

"Are you wearing makeup, Princess Ryan?"

I cross my arms in front of my chest.

"Sir. We are going to a bar. Thought it best if I at least tried to fit in."

He comes around the table and throws an arm over my shoulder, while handing me a set of keys. He pulls me in close so my ear is next to his mouth.

"Good Idea, Ryan. Blending in with...girls."

I elbow him in the ribs, not holding back.

"Nice. You'll really fit in with punches like that," He tells me.

He turns back when he reaches the door, "C'mon. The rest of the guys should be here any minute."

Out in the parking lot the guys trickle in. First Daniels, then Kelley, T-Rex, Peppers, Meaty and Hanzo. I feel a bubble of disappointment that Broussard isn't among the group. I squash that feeling down as soon as I recognize it and reach for the handle of the driver's side door. T-Rex is next to me suddenly, pushing my hand away, while opening it for himself to get in. T-Rex is by far the biggest guy on the team, but he turns around when he realizes I haven't moved to the passenger side.

"Get in, Princess. A'int no woman I'll let drive me when I'm sober."

"Ha. You can drive if you can get the keys from me, and we all know I'm faster then you."

I dodge out of his lunge range.

Reed yells from his position in the front passenger seat, "C'mon T! All the rest of us are ready to go, pussies are waiting, drinks are chillin."

T-Rex makes another half lunge at me. I laugh and dance back from him. I can see the frustration in his eyes. Whoops, this is getting real – I am teasing the bear.

The guys start getting restless and start chanting, "Get in. Get in. Get in."

On the third unsuccessful attempt of taking the keys from me, T throws his hands up and walks to the other side of the van and gets in. I make sure his door is closed and he is buckled before sliding in the driver's seat.

I put the van in reverse and turn around to watch as I back the behemoth out of it's spot. The guy's faces are a comical mix of eagerness for tonight's entertainment, trepidation at letting me drive and quiet don't-say-anything-in-front-of-the-girl mentality.

I ease down on the gas a little, then abruptly hit the brakes. Silence reigns in the van. I start laughing. This is just too comical. These men.

I put the van in gear and put the pedal to the metal so to speak.

I yell at them, "Loosen up, Pussies! I promise you'll enjoy the ride!"

The van is slow to gain any speed with it's cumbersome load of seven heavy-hitting SEALs and minimal engine power- but we were off.

9

The first bar we go to is just off Water Street in Norfolk. It is a hole in the wall kind of place, and I think the best part about it is that you can see the ships parked across the river. There are a few patrons when we arrive, and I suck soda water and lime while the guys down beers and play pool. They have a dartboard, and eventually the quietness of the bar has me up and throwing darts just to ease the bit or restlessness inside me.

Thankfully, (or maybe unfortunately) the bar never picks up, and we have been there an hour. So we load up and head further inland to an Irish pub called Flynn's. It is livelier with a raucous mixed crowd of men and women. The guys order drinks and stand around the bar, while I move deeper into the crowd hoping to snag a booth or high top table- but the chances look slim in this crowd.

When I reach the end of the bar, I literally bump into an old marine buddy- my shoulder to his chest- as he had quickly spun around from where he was standing at the bar with his group.

"Holy Shit. Everly Ryan. What the fuck you doing here?" is Shawn Connolly's greeting.

"Chip, you fucker!" I practically yell it in my excitement- but in the crowded room it seems to be the right pitch for him to hear. I give him a hug and pull away while faking a punch at his jaw. He playfully dodges.

I had chipped Shawn's tooth back when we were in the marines. We were playing some drinking game that involved throwing punches to see who could bleed first. The guys hadn't wanted me to play, but I persuaded them, and threw the first punch hitting Shawn square in the face. He bled and my knuckles bled. We both tossed back a shot and laughed about it. We were instant friends from there on out. Shawn is in Spec ops. Just like I had been trained to be in.

"I can't believe you're here. Shit! Let me buy you a drink."

"I'm actually here…" How could I explain this? Shawn only knew I had not re-enlisted with the Marines after my four years because of family. I had never explained to anyone how I got into BUD/S and I wasn't going to start now. But how could I explain that I was here with my team, when it was top secret that I had even completed BUD/S and was now training with a team?

I involuntarily turn around and look down the bar. The guys had commandeered a booth back behind the pool tables, and while most of them were there, Reed was standing directly behind me with a beer in his hand and looking at me quizzically.

He raises an eyebrow in question while lifting the bottle to his lips.

I turn back to Shawn. He had seen me make eye contact with Reed.

"Shit! You're here with a sailor!"

I don't know how he pegged Reed so quick, but obviously this situation requires some special extraction skills.

"Hey Connolly. It's not like that. "

His blue eyes look down at me.

"Yea, it's not like that." A shit-eating grin spreads across his face.

He pushes past me and zeroes in on Reed. Pulling up in front of him he thrusts his hand out to shake.

"Sir, Shawn Connolly, U.S. Marines."

Shaking the hand that was offered him, Reed responds, "Reed. U.S. Navy. How do you know our girl here?"

I didn't miss the "our girl." It is perplexing and thrilling to think they might finally be treating me as one of the team.

I fill in the blanks, "We served together in the Marines."

"Aha. Yes…" Reed starts, " Come meet the rest of the team."

What follows is a pool battle royal between some of Shawn's marine buddies and my new team.

I am nursing my third soda water with lime, when Reed finishes his turn at the pool table. He slides in the booth across from Shawn and I, who had been conversing over past shenanigans.

"…Remember how we were on that training mission in Guam and Cruz fell out of the boat?"

I snorted. "How could I forget?"

I glanced up at Reed who is practically eye fucking a blonde at the bar. She has her back to the pool tables and unlike certain other ladies of the bar, seems to be ignoring our group. Which for a person of the female persuasion has got to be the hardest thing in the world to do. Besides the size of the guys themselves, when put together an air of strength and confidence pervades any room they are in.

I decide to needle Reed just a little bit.

"Yo, Reed. You get her number yet? Or you just gonna stare at her all night?"

He turns back to me and flips me the bird.

This sends Shawn into peals of laughter. He slides out of the booth to get another beer and take his turn at the pool table.

Reed is already back staring at the blonde. I do a cursory inspection.

She is dressed classy. Black pencil skirt, teal silk blouse, jacket draped across the back of her bar stool. Nursing a glass of white wine. Classy, but on the prowl.

"You want a pointer," I ask Reed and continue on without his affirmative, "Go up there and tell her you think her Louboutins are sexy as fuck."

"And what exactly is a Louboutin?" he fairly growls at me.

"It's a designer shoe. And she's wearing them."

He looks at me skeptically.

"How do you know?"

"It's the red sole of the shoe. It's the Louboutin trademark."

Without further ado, he slides out of the booth. Takes two steps and turns back to me.

"If this doesn't work- you owe me Ryan."

"Only one way to find out."

I watch as he approaches the girl. He puts one hand on the bar by her drink and turns his body so they are almost touching.
Cagey bastard. He has his own moves.

T-Rex slides in the seat next to me as I watch Reed's drama unfold. T had drunk about twelve beers in the last three hours and still seems sober.

"What's going on over there?"

"Reed's using my line to pick up that chick."

We both watch as Reed leans in, and puts his lips at her ear. She pulls back and starts laughing. They chat a bit more, and then she pulls out her feet out from under the barstool and shows off her shoes to Reed. He must give the appropriate compliments as she then signals the bartender to get them another round.

I roll my eyes at how easy that was.

10

A text message wakes me the next day.
Command post – 2100. Pre-training briefing.

Command post was just our office- and well it was odd that we would have meeting at night on a Saturday, there are weirder things.

I opened command's door ten minutes before nine. Reed and Peppers are already there, their beers leaving sweat rings on the conference table.

"Hey. Reed, Peppers."

Just as I lay my hand on the back of a chair to pull it out and sit down, Reed comments, "Ryan. go to my office and bring me the bottle that's in the second drawer."

I am the grunt, and grunts always get the grunt work.

"Sure thing."

I hop to and make quick time to his desk in the side office.

The second drawer holds a full bottle of whiskey. Might as well grab the shot glass that is sitting next to it.

When I re-enter the conference room T-Rex and Meaty are there in addition to Reed and Peppers. Meaty still looks a bit hung over.

I place the bottle at Reed's right hand.

He leans back in his chair and pushes the chair next to him out with his foot; an invitation for me to take a seat. It is between him and Peppers. A Cheshire grin spreads across his face.

"Sit down Ryan. "

Not totally trusting, I take the chair he has so gallantly offered with his foot.

I am reading mischievousness off these three – Meaty isn't included because his head is currently laid out on the table in his arms.

"Peppers," Reed begins, "Don't you think it's time we initiated Petty Officer Ryan here into the ranks of Seal Team X? "

Peppers smiles a gamine grin.

"Without a doubt, sir."

"We shall proceed then. T-Rex. The honors please."

T-Rex had been making his way around the conference table, trying to be nonchalant. But at his size, he has been doing a good imitation of an elephant circling a watering hole.

As I lift my butt from my seat, to dodge whatever attack he is aiming my way, his hands come down on my shoulders and push me back down into the chair.

"Petty officer Ryan is charged with…" Reed lets his hand trail in the air as he ponders my charge.

"Pimping."

I laugh.

"Pimping?" I question back at him.

Reed pretends to stroke a non-existent goatee while his eyes narrow in regard to me.

"Do you know one Jessica St. Clair?"

"No."

"Take a shot of whiskey," he says while pushing the bottle towards my hand.

I unscrew the cap. Hazing comes with any team territory. Do I trust them enough to lift this bottle to my lips?

I do. With only the slightest hesitation I lift the bottle to my lips without breaking eye contact with Reed. I take a healthy swallow.

It burns on the way down. But, I am proud of myself for not coughing.

I carefully place the bottle back on the table.

T-Rex is still standing menacingly - or so he thinks- behind my chair.

Hanzo abruptly enters the conference room. He comes in and places his medic bag on the table. Very dramatic without any greetings.

T-Rex unrolls a strip of duct tape from behind me. The sound of the tape ripping is meant as a threat and I take it as one. The guys are doing their best to intimidate me.

Reed takes the whiskey bottle from my left hand and places it against his lips. After his swig, he puts it back at my hand deliberately.

"You see, Petty Officer Ryan, we just want to make sure your intentions are one hundred and fifty fucking present copacetic with the team."

As he is speaking T-Rex places a strip of duct tape over my right arm where it rests on the arm of the chair. He follows the first strip up with a complete roll over and under my arm with the tape.

I don't flinch. I watch him do it with a strange curiosity. Wondering to myself what these boys are up to. They probably hope I'll wuss out and the game will be over. Then they'd do everything they could to see me off the team.

I look up from T-Rex's work- where he is duct taping my right foot to one of the spokes of the rolling chair.

I'll be on board with whatever torture they have to dole out if it means they'll start to accept me as one of the team.

I smile and lift my head.

"Reed. Something tells me this is nothing to do with your hook up last night at the bar."
"Take a shot of whiskey."

My free left hand reaches out and snags the neck of the bottle, lifting it to my lips.

The heat curls deliciously in my belly this time- no burn.

What progresses is a question and answer session, which I only seem to remember flashes of.

After my fourth swig, I believe T-Rex duct-taped my shoulders to the back of the chair. After the sixth (or was it seventh?), Peppers brought out the clippers.

There was a large struggle after that, and I believe I managed to hold my own against the four men claiming I was, "too pretty to be a SEAL."

I was too tired to fight (and really fight is a loose term to describe how I moved my body weight in the chair hoping to dislodge four grown —and trained in combat— men) when the vibration of the clippers hit the side of my skull.

Let them do their worst. I had shaved my head before and if they believe I am vain enough to miss a few locks, they're going to be disappointed.

I close my eyes when they are done. The prick of Hanzo setting up an IV treatment a little later isn't even enough to really rouse me. I watch him slide the needle into a vein in my arm, but I am too numb to do more then close my eyes and surrender to oblivion.

Hanzo says, "This is the fastest way to sober up with no hangover, Ryan. You can thank me tomorrow."

I let my head tip backward on the chair, staring up at the fluorescents until they start to fade.

11

Broussard

Sunday morning I'm awake at four thirty like clockwork. I throw on shorts and wander out to my balcony with a cup of coffee. I'd been in this apartment for four months, since Miranda and I had separated at the end of my last deployment. Just two more months, and I'll have to put what little furniture I have back into storage when we go out again. I am a little tired of the shuffle, so I let my brain switch gears to work, organizing and tasking things I have to do before our Monday morning bug out.

The wind is up, the air has a chill to it. I do some quick push-ups and jump in the shower.

Arriving at the office a little over an hour later. No cars in the parking lot, and the usual tranquility of a Sunday morning sunrise permeates the air. This is my favorite time of day. I savor it a moment.

I pull open the office door and input my security code. The lights are still on in the conference room. I reach my hand through the door with the intention of just shutting the lights off and continuing on to my office, but something doesn't feel right.

I use my shoulder to push the door open more.

There. At the backside of the conference table is…Ryan duct taped to a chair. I know from the slight form and dainty shape of the face. My eyes immediately scan the area for any other threats. None.

I waste no time moving to her side to feel at her neck for a pulse.

It's there and strong. A piece of duct tape covers her mouth. Her head tipped over the back of the chair, eyes closed.

I lift her head and gray eyes open and blink at me.

I yank the strip of duct tape from her mouth.

"Unnh…" is her thanks.

It is then that I pull my hand from the back of her head. The softness of her hair is unreal and also, curiously cropped, scalp-short on one side.

Duct taped to the wall next to her is an IV bag with its long cord disappearing into her right arm. I know what's happened here – good 'ole welcome to the team ritual.

"Jesus, Ryan. Are you alright?"

She is now alternating looking at me and down at her situation.

"Unnnh….yea…really got to pee…."

How long has she been like this? I grab my pocketknife from the side pocket on my cargo shorts. I slice in the negative space between her right arm and the chair arm. For the next few minutes we are both silent as I work on her legs and her left arm.

As I work, I let the shock and annoyance go. Really, I shouldn't have been so surprised, being a part of the team comes with it's own rituals and hazing that Everly Ryan has yet to be subjected to because she is a girl. These things happen all the time in the normal course of things, and I had even participated in several "welcome to the team" meetings myself.

So what if the other guys on the team had finally given in to the reality that Petty Officer Everly Ryan is a member of Seal Team Four?

She's one of us. A team member. I am uncharacteristically pissed, worried and…proud? I concentrate on the task at hand –pulling duct tape first from her ankles, then her thighs while ignoring the emotions. I can deal with those later.

Once I cut her left arm and hand free, she grabs the IV going into her right wrist and yanks it free. I am still working at the duct tape holding her shoulders down to the back of the computer chair.

She reaches up and yanks the duct tape across her torso, before I can slice it with my pocket knife.

"Thank you, Sir."

She catapults from the chair and leaves me holding some wadded up strips of duct tape in one hand and my pocketknife in the other.

Ryan

I hardly spare Broussard a glance. My urge to pee is so monumental that I knew if I took a deep breath my bladder will release.

Once I had relieved myself in the bathroom, I wash my hands at the sink and let the momentary embarrassment of Broussard finding me wash over me.

Running my hands beneath the faucet and splashing some water on my face helps me clear the fogginess from my brain. I confront my reflection in the mirror.

Not too bad. Except the jagged shave spot from beneath my ear to the top of my head on the right side.

I dip my hands underneath the stream again and do an internal scan of my body.

No hangover. Just seriously jacked hair. I tilt my head to the left and run my palm up the freshly shorn side.

An awesome idea flashes through my brain. It'd kick ass and glee skitters up my spine in anticipation.

This will show the guys after I'm sure what they're thinking will have me tucking tail and running from their "haircut" last night.

I just need to get out of the office without further run-ins with any of the team- Broussard included, maybe most especially Broussard.

I open the bathroom door, go down the short hall, and peek around the doorway into the conference room. The duct tape chair is still there, looking like a caterpillar has emerged from its tape shell. That's what I'd be. Before- a caterpillar; after –a bad ass. The guys have unwittingly fueled my motivation at a time when I was seriously questioning everything.

Thank Christ – No Broussard.

I tiptoe as silently and as quietly as I can to the front door. The heavy metal screeches as I pull it open, but I quickly skirt through it and shut it behind me.

Broussard's Jeep is the only vehicle in the parking lot. Good.

No witnesses to see my temporary retreat.

Broussard

I let Ryan escape the office without any further humiliation. Knowing when she left by only hearing the outside door shut behind her.

I dial Reed on my phone. If any one knew the scoop it'd most likely be him.

12

The Monday morning bug out was scheduled for 0500. After a short meeting, we'd gear up and load up. This particular training mission was a simple drop in, secure, and bug out. After my conversation with Reed yesterday, I thought it couldn't hurt to bring Ryan in on this one. See how she got along with the rest of the team on an op. Maybe I could finally get command to see what a liability it is having her on the team. Well, not her personally. Just a woman in general.

I pull my laptop out of my bag and connect it to the projector we use in briefings. As the team is filtering in, I pull up my email and scroll through the different messages absentmindedly.

I had watched Everly Ryan whenever we did PT, during meetings and on base trainings- including a hand to hand combat refresher course we did just two weeks ago. She always proves her mettle. Some things she is better at then the guys- speed and agility- but other things are just not equal. Strength being one.

I remember her fierce expression when she had paired up with T-Rex in the ring for some hand-to-hand. She had managed to get in several good jabs, but when she threw a

47

kick, T-Rex caught it. The resounding thud her butt made when it hit the mat had me cringing. She took it like a champ though, popping back up and decking T in the chin. He got lucky when she came in close for a punch one time, and he put her in a headlock till she passed out. She didn't tap out though. She blacked out and the bruising around her neck was a purple testimony that she had withstood hand to hand with a man nearly double her size.

I had been watching her with a scrutiny meant to only find a solution to the problem she presented. She was quiet. But not in a mousy, shy girl way. Her silence was strength, bold, determination- stoic. Her gray eyes observe everything in her sphere with the same intense gaze a hawk uses on a hunt. At the same time though, she is efficient and anticipates my needs whenever she acts as team liaison.

The words on her bio from the psych analysis she had submitted to before BUD/S are etched on my mind, mainly because I had read it several hundred times trying to find a weakness I could exploit. The report read, *Hardly a feminist. The inner determination Petty Officer Ryan exhibits is in direct relation to her commitment to save lives and be there for her fellow brethren. When questioned further about her feelings- no answer. Only an unswerving loyalty to men-in-arms. "In war, gender has no place, but love of country and ability to do the job do. I can and will do this job."*

There had to be something further. Something I could use to finish this experiment. It's probably the only time I ever wanted to fail. A woman in active combat, stealth operations…it's not only a risk to her life, but to everyone else's. Nothing to do with her ability to do the job. But it sure as well affects mine, because god knows my traditional upbringing can only provide one answer on what to do with her in a combat situation. Protect her. Those instincts will be hard to quash in a direct action.

Reed interrupts my musings.

"It's 0500, sir. Time to saddle up and ride."

He plunks down next to me. Most of the team is seated at the conference table or standing up in various positions along the wall. I scanned the faces.

Missing one. I am now curious if the guys had managed to scare Ryan off with their scare tactics Saturday night. Guess now I know.

Huh. Disappointment flashes in my gut, didn't think it'd be so easy.

I disregard it. Briefing now. Emotions later…if I ever decide to pluck them from the depths of my mind and examine them.

"Alright Team. We got a simple drop in here…"

I trail off as movement by the door catches my eye.

It is Ryan. And she has a Mohawk. A fucking Mohawk. Dyed black, not her signature honey brown I am used to. It isn't the highest Mohawk or the traditionally spikey kind, but it is two inches tall and smoothed up to the center of her head.

She has also done something with her makeup- hell, I never knew she ever wore any- that was downright scary. Eyeliner as dark as midnight, and under the fluorescent lighting her eyes met mine- electric blue and disconcerting to me – as I was used to her gray intelligent eyes. But these…these are sex eyes. That thought has me snapping back to reality.

"Ryan. Glad you took time fix your hair and makeup for this beauty pageant."

Snickers break out around the room. She nonchalantly leans against the wall in parade rest.

"Listen up, Ryan. Today you're trading your tiara for a helmet. Standard recon force 5. I want a team here and a team insert here."

The details are on instant replay in my head so regurgitating them comes naturally even though my attention is on little Miss Attitude leaning against the wall in the back.

With a, "Lock and load ladies!" the briefing breaks up on my command.

Good 'ole sexual attraction. I snuff it out, put such feelings to the back of my mind, never to see the light of day again- or so I hope.

13

Ryan

I'm keeping this Mohawk. It is lucky. My lucky Mohawk. First day I have it I get to go on a training op.

I really have no assigned role on the op- just a back-up gun so to speak. But, I get to parachute from the C-130 and be in the field. It feels fucking fantastic.

It took us close to three hours to hike covertly to our package location. The takedown - uneventful. But my spirit could not be dampened. I had boots on the ground and a M16 in my grip. The only reason I don't grin from ear to ear is because I think it might be uncool. Keep it together Ryan.

We reach the extract point and a UH-60 (that's a Blackhawk helicopter) is waiting for us.

We load up without issues. I am squashed between T-Rex and Reed. For some reason the guys think because I am smaller (or maybe just female) I'll fit best on the jump seat next to T-Rex. Not really. With all our gear, and the fact that I have hips, we are touching from shoulder to knee- with the butt of our rifles resting on the ground between our feet. It is as fun as being squashed next to...well, the carnivorous dinosaur T is named after.

Still, Reed is amicable and charming.

"So, Ryan," he shouts over the cha, cha, cha of the rotating blades, "You got any fashion tips for me?"

I glance at him.

"You Asshole." I yell back. I'm sure my words carry on the wind, cause T-Rex guffaws.

"I was just wondering," he continues, "If Louboutin makes a combat boot in my size. I think the red heel would be a nice target spot for any tangos."

I start laughing at the image of a Louboutin combat boot.

"Maybe you can ask your girlfriend to pick you out a pair...." Just as I say it, I realize how that sounds. T-Rex breaks in, "Yea a pair of balls.
YOUPUSSYMOTHERFUCKER! "

Ha! I am starting to like T.

We banter back and forth the whole ride back to the airfield.

Hoo-Yah. It feels damn good to be back in the saddle.

Broussard

It is hard to keep my eyes off her. She kept a game face on during the whole training, but the minute the exit helo took off, it seems that her eyes are gleaming with success. Unbridled happiness. A soul-deep fire reflected in her eyes. And I know. She has the heart of a warrior. Gets off on this shit just as much as I do.

I try my best to not pay any attention to her- but I kept finding my gaze roving her way. She chats back and forth between T-Rex and Reed, playfully punching T in the arm, then throwing back her head in laughter. Her eyes are dewy with victory and ringed in battle paint.

Probably not even a regulation on that shit.

She is dwarfed by T-Rex on her left side, and the contrast in their sizes really hits home her femininity. While her feminine shape doesn't exist in full gear, her lack of size sitting next to T-Rex is apparent- her nose would bump into the top of his shoulder if she turned her head. Still she keeps talking, now gesturing something flippant with a backward wave of her hand. T-Rex responds - I can't hear what they were saying over the wind- but Ryan's lips stretch into a relaxed grin as she leans the back of her head against the bulkhead.

"Yo, Broussie." Hanzo leans into my right side so I can hear him, "what you think of Ryan?"

I watch her face a second longer.

"I don't know Hanz. I think things would just be a lot simpler if she wasn't a she."

Yea. If she wasn't a she I wouldn't be attracted to her.

"Yea, Chief. She can pull her weight, but let's be honest. She's a girl. And that's complicated."

I pulled my eyes from her. Back out the door of the copter.

"Yea, Hanzo, you know us SEALs hate fucking complications."

He laughs at that and all too soon we are making our descent back to base.

14

Ryan

I am slowly fitting in with the team, letting them get to know me, getting to know them. In addition to Reed and T-Rex, I have also thawed Hanzo and Meaty enough that when they break out in their man talk there is enough camaraderie with them to be included as just one of the guys.

I haven't cracked the nut that is Chief Broussard, though. He sticks to my ass anytime we are on training missions and he never breaks his professional mask to get personal. SEAL ranks are nebulous in the unofficial capacity. It has more to do with a respect earned seniority system than an actual official rank. And the CO has more respect than anyone else.

I keep that respect by keeping my distance for the most part. It is on a Tuesday in April, just two weeks before our deployment that some of that distance closes between us. The team is seated around the conference table and I think some of the guys still had hangovers from whatever entertainment they sought the night before.. T-Rex has sporting a bruise on his jaw, probably a remnant of a drunken bar fight, and I wonder how his wife feels when he comes home with that. I switch my mind to the Broussard briefing us on the training mission -a launch from a submarine. I can feel the fear skirt up my spine as I get the details. We all have fears, and my biggest one is claustrophobia. I've confronted it a couple times before, but still hate small spaces.

"...And our extract point is five miles from the sub..." Broussard finishes up.

"Ryan, you got that?"

'Yes sir."

Even though I had it, I felt swirl of fear in my gut. I hate fucking subs. Ironic since I am in the Navy – and every ship and submarine is comprised of the smallest of small spaces.

Broussard

In the dry dock before my team deploys to the surface I am studying maps and not my team. After all, this type of training mission I have done at least a dozen times before and my team – at least half a dozen. It is my mistake not to be watching the rookies. I should always be keeping my eye on Ryan.

We are in the holding tank of the sub when T-Rex calls my name.

"Yo! Chief. A word."

"Not now, T-Rex. We have less than three minutes to launch!"

I don't even look up from my map.

"Sir. Please- it's imperative."

His quiet words reverberate off the bulkheads. Barely heard over the water coming in the inlets at our feet. It is a task to get down his end of the tank- full gear and all.

But once I do, I immediately see the problem. Ryan is hyperventilating and hardly aware that I have sat on the bench across from her.

Shit. She'd never make it to the surface in this condition.

"T- you partner with Reed. I'll take Ryan, and give us your back."

T immediately turns his body and it shields Ryan from the rest of the team.

I pull her hands from where they are clenched in her lap.

Her eyes are fixated at the water swirling at my calves.

"Listen up Ryan." I pull her goggles down over eyes and pull her regulator over her shoulder.

Her eyes are near vacant, and I tap her chin to get her to look at me.

"Ryan. Nod your head yes that you can hear me."

She does, in a barely perceptible dip of her chin.

"I've got you to the surface. You're going to be ok – I've got you. All I need you to do is breathe in and out and follow my lead. Got it?"

Her eyes are darting to one side and another looking at the water at my knees now.

"Listen to my voice Ryan. Look at me."

She does and our eyes lock. I know this is the crucial time- if I can I get her to beat back her fear- we'll have no problems.

"Just breathe. Follow me."

I take a deep breath and exhale. One more. Two more, than three.

Ryan is focused on me, our eye contacting never breaking. I put the regulator up to her mouth, because now, the water is up to my hips. Soon, the water will be over our heads and the bulkhead doors will open, releasing us to complete our mission.

She puts the regulator in her mouth and adjusts her goggles.

She seems to be on an even keel now, but still has the water rises, I hold her hand and make sure her breathing is in sync with my own.

When the bulkhead doors open and we are the last to swim out, I let go of her hand but signal that she is to follow me. She nods and we begin swimming.

Our mission is to scuba to a ship a mile out, place underwater charges and then swim to an extraction point- just a sandbar in the sea.

Once we are at the ship, Ryan places her charges without prompting from me, and we take off without anymore issues.

I'm swimming to the extraction, the wheels are turning in my head. This is what I could use to get Ryan off the team. She could fucking compromise a whole mission with whatever that panic attack shit is she just pulled.

Reaching the surface – I wait till Ryan does too, and then swim in tandem with her to the beach. I keep silent until my feet hit the sand. I pull Ryan in a bit roughly by her tank straps, not giving her a chance to get her own feet under her.

"You care to explain what happened, Ryan?" She pulls away without a word and plops down in the sand to pull her flippers off. Her goggles are pushed back on her head. It's a cold night, our breaths are puffing out in little clouds illuminated by the half moon.

"No, I do not care to explain."

I check the GPS on my wrist, we have about a three mile walk to the extraction point. I look at her.

"Fine. I order you to tell me what your fucking problem was before we launched."

She jumps up and in my face, the scent of her soap or shampoo or whatever reaches my nostrils and I am in a moment of insanity where I visualize laying her down on the beach and pounding my dick into her. Her quick finger jab into my chest tells me that she's gone full offensive/defensive mode, and it notches up my anger and sex drive another degree.

"It's not your fucking business, Broussard."

I grab her wrist and look into her eyes.

"It sure as shit is my business when you can't complete the mission," I tell her quietly.

She jerks her hand out of my grasp and I let her. Picking up her tank and flippers she begins walking.

Fine by me. I could use a minute to calm down myself. A half-mile passes in which we walk in silence. I see the dark shapes of the other team members on the beach ahead of us.

"You going to tell me, Ryan? Or I got to go to the higher-ups with this one?"

She's quiet a minute. But then her voice resolutely says, "It's claustrophobia. I'm…Claustrophobic. I've never…It's never been like that before."

A panic attack brought on by claustrophobia. I don't say anything else to her, just quietly join the team and wait for pickup.

Ryan

Showing vulnerability…it's not something I do, ever. I hate it. Everyone seems to sense the tension between the chief and I, the debriefing is quick and lacking the usual banter. As we break up to go our separate ways, Reed asks me, "Yo! Ryan. You down for a good 'ole honky-tonk time?"

"You asking me out, Reed?"

"Jessica wants to meet you and a few of the guys from the team." He replies.

"Well, far be it for me to deny the lovely Jessica."

T-Rex snorts beside me.

"Hey fuck-face, you should bring Jordan too." I tell him.

58

"Oh, trust me. I already got my orders to do so." He gives Reed a thanks-a-lot face.

I'm one hundred percent in. I need alcohol to forget what I admitted to Chief Broussard. I need alcohol to forget how he helped me focus, calmed me down. How his eyes struck into my heart and gave me courage. How we argued on the beach.

"All right, when and where?" I get the details from Reed.

It's how I find myself in probably the only western-themed bar on the eastern seaboard.

15

My limited wardrobe had to suffice, and in theme it
wasn't: leather jacket, black t-shirt, jeans, and cross trainers.
Amid the cowboy boots and western-style shirts it seemed I
was the odd-man-out. Thankfully, T and I had dressed
damn near similar. His wife, Jordan though, she embraced
the theme with a chambray shirt, skin-tight jeans, and
honest-to-god cowboy boots.

I asked her about them while I sipped on my first beer.

"Yeah, picked 'em up in Austin last year. Every girl
needs a good pair of shit-kickers." She replied.

"Huh." is all I could reply. Running through my brain
were my own pair of boots, cross trainers and shower
shoes. Shit-kickers, yes. But did they make my butt look as
good as this girl's? I doubt it. Maybe it was time I upgraded
my shoe collection- or lack thereof. Does Broussard find
women in high heels sexy?

I quickly shook my head. Yea. I definitely needed to
switch to a hard liquor. I left our table and saddled up to
the bar.

I noticed the looks I got- sure. My height put me
above most of the female population- a gargantuan gazelle
among lions. The advantage: the bartender acknowledged
me almost immediately when I reached the bar.

I placed my order, "A kamikaze...And a vodka tonic."

I downed the shot when it was placed in front of me and sipped the drink while the bartender ran my card.

He returned with my card and another shot.

"It's on the house, gorgeous." He gave me a wink.

I picked it up and downed it. "Thanks."

I made my way back to our table, where the guys and their girls were chatting away.

"Whoa-hoo. Ryan! Hitting the hard stuff already?"

I tipped my glass to Reed's greeting.

"Damn right," I told him, "I need something to prep me for this…" I waved my hand in the air, "… line dancing."

Jessica clapped her hands together and squealed.

That was my sign, tonight was going to hell in a hand basket.

Broussard

Something was dragging my from the deep slumber I was in. A ringing. I rolled over, my phone was glowing blue on the nightstand. I grabbed it and swiped right to accept the call from Reed.

"Broussard, go."

"Chief. We got a problem."

I sat up and clicked the bedside light on.

"Yea?"

T-Rex and Ryan got in a brawl. T's already out, I'm taking him and the girls home. But they won't release Ryan till they talk to her commander."

"She alright?" I ask him.

"Yea, chief. Just some typical asshole bullshit."

I ran my hand through my hair and pulled on the pair of jeans I had left draped on the footboard of the bed.

"Where is she at?"

"The townies out here in Princess Ann got her. It's a small outfit. Shouldn't be hard to spring her."

I pulled a shirt over my head and looked around for my car keys.

"And what exactly did she do?"

Silence for beat. "She just got between T-Rex and an asshole. The asshole apparently is some muckity-muck's son or something."

"Where exactly is she at?"

I get the details and gather up my keys and wallet. Even though I just rolled out of bed, I throw a button up shirt on over my t-shirt. Wouldn't hurt to look respectable when you have to break someone out of jail.

Thank god the local law enforcement were accommodating when one of our sailors gets out of line. They'll usually let us take over punishment for the civil disobedience knowing our justice would usually be quicker and harder.

Ryan

The holding cell had four other occupants. One girl passed out drunk, a couple of crack or meth heads, and one girl I was pretty sure was hooker. I didn't talk to them. Surely, Reed would be here soon to get me out. An hour passed. I laid my head against the wall and closed my eyes. The alcohol was wearing off enough to leave me with a headache and dry mouth.

"Ryan! You're up!" A guard's shout breaks the silence.

I cross through the door and back into the processing office.

"Today's your lucky day, girl. Charges are dropped," says the processing officer. He's got a paunch from too many beers on his off day and sitting behind a desk.

He hands me a baggie that contains my credit card, cash, I.D., and shoe laces.

"You can exit through here. And remember, stay out of trouble, girlie."

He gives me a wink. I wasn't really sure what to make of that.

I stepped through the door he indicated and saw Chief Broussard sitting in a chair apparently waiting on me.

His eyes scan me from head to toe. Pause on my fat lip. His eyes narrow.

I can read the question in the lift of his eyebrow and answer it before he can voice it.

"Got in the way of an elbow," I tell him.

He grunts. Makes his way to the door. I fall in step behind him.

His jeep is parked at the curb.

We both get in without a word.

I buckle up while he reverses. His warm masculine scent envelopes our space in intimacy. I ignore it.

While we drive down the highway, I notice his hands on the steering wheel. Strong and without a wedding ring. A flutter in my stomach. My brain rationalizes that he probably just takes it off sometimes.

"Ryan," Broussard breaks the silence, "You should know better than that. I had to pull some major strings back there and the higher ups are not happy that two of my team got arrested tonight. Shit- I'm not happy."

I don't really know how to answer. I let the alcohol make a dumb decision for me. To step between T-Rex and a little snot nosed college kid… that was not using my brain power.

"You're right," I tell him, "it was completely uncalled for- I shouldn't have done it. God knows T-Rex can defend himself."

Broussard looks to me, studies my face as if he is trying to determine my sincerity.

"I should, by all rights, start your discharge paperwork Ryan."

I don't say anything to his statement. Maybe he is right. I fucked up. It didn't feel good and shame kept me quiet.

"Nothing to say?" he questions.

"No sir." I reply.

His hand slams down on the steering wheel and he brakes hard, slams the car into park. I brace my hands on the dash.

"Fuck! WHAT THE FUCK ARE YOU THINKING? HUH? YOU'RE JUST ONE OF THE GUYS?" He shouts angrily without looking in my direction.

I am frozen. I've never seen such an outburst from the chief. Don't know what to make of it. The headlights from the car shine on the dirt shoulder in front of us. No cars are passing and I just listen to Broussard's breathing a minute.

His quiet voice breaks into the tense silence, "You are not one of the guy's Ryan. It'd be best if you accept that sooner rather than later."

He puts the jeep into drive, and I don't acknowledge his statement.

We ride silently back to the barracks. I don't know how he knows what building I'm in, but when he pulls to a stop in front of it, I unbuckle quickly and pull on the handle.

Just as my foot swings out the door, his voice makes me pause.

"I hate the fucking silent treatment, Ryan."

I only have one response, "Yes sir."

He's looking straight out of the front window.

I've been over there eight tours, Ryan. I know what it takes. What it'll do to you. I'm not saying you have to give up; we can transfer you to a non-combat position. Hell, I'll advocate for a special support personnel spot so you can still be with the team."

I squash my immediate reaction of annoyance. He doesn't understand. He wants me on the sidelines just like everyone else. But my gut is telling me it's because for some reason more than because I'm a girl.

I step out onto the curb and close the door of the jeep.

"Thanks for the ride, Chief." I close the door and he pulls away. I handled that badly. I should've been more respectful, pleaded my case to him, been more grateful for the pickup- I know his rank and position are probably the only reason I won't be in front of a judge on Monday morning.

PART II

Charlie Foxtrot

16

We are a month into deployment. Middle east and the boredom is enough to drive me bat shit crazy. The boys have an X-box or some shit in their bunkhouse (and bunkhouse is a generous term for the plywood construction pods set up as our temporary barracks) that they play to keep from going totally crazy. Me? I've been running and running. It's late afternoon, and I've been out just thirty minutes. Kicking up dust clouds as the sun sinks, I give a half wave to the guard tower as I go round the interior of the base. Turning a corner, I spot a figure in my path, so I slow, not wanting to run them down.

As I get closer, I notice that it's one of the CIA agents I've seen around the base. I give him a noncommittal nod while trying to puzzle out what he's doing in my running path.

"Ryan, right?"

I pause in front of him. A trickle of alarm flickers in my brain. I ignore it. CIA is on our side. I place one hand on my hip and wipe the sweat off my brow with the other.

"Yea. I'm Ryan. And you are…?"

A sudden darkness blinks out the sunset's orange glow, and I throw my hands up while running forward. I crash into the solidness of his body, and we both go to the ground. A sharp elbow (or something) clips my left temple and I see yellow fireflies. A knee in my back pins me to the ground, while my arms are snatched behind me in a standard yet painful-restraint.

I'm still trying my best to break out of the hold- bucking my hips and straining my shoulder muscles- when a sharp stabbing pain erupts in my right thigh.

Fuck. They've stabbed me.

The shock of it freezing me mid-fight.

Fight, Fight, Fight.

But my muscles seem disconnected from my body, dead and unmoving.

Blackness is creeping into my vision.

Not stabbed. Drugged...

Broussard

"Yo! T-Rex. You seen Ryan this morning? She missed PT and the 0900 briefing."

I've got the team split into two groups, that rotate PT and training time, to keep things interesting. We've been deployed and are just waiting on orders for any type of orders we might be needed for.

I've tracked T-Rex down in the mess tent, and was sure if anyone knew if Ryan was sick it'd be him. These two are tighter then two peas in a pod here lately.

He pauses with a forkful of mashed potatoes halfway to his mouth.

"No. Chief. I thought you had her on some special go- fer."

Well, this is perplexing. It's not like Ryan to pull a failure to report.

If she was sick, surely she'd call in to Hanzo or the XO.

I leave the mess hall and make quick work to the girl's barracks.

This time of the day, there shouldn't be too many people about, but I still announce my presence with a knock and, "Ladies- Dick on Deck- Watch it!"

There were only a few females in residence on base, but I'm not sure what I'll encounter here.

The girls have small compartments, and I only know I'm at Ryan's by the spray paint announcement on the door, "Ryan - 10E." I knock and without an answer, push open the door. I take a look around. Her bed is made. Boots tucked in at the end. So wherever she is, she's either wearing shower flip-flops or cross trainers.

Her Boston Red Sox's cap is clipped to the head rail. Other then that, her locker is closed and no extra clues are lying about.

I exit and walk the short hallway to the bunk compartment next to hers.

Knock on the door, no answer.

Going on down the line, I don't get an answer till the fourth door. A dark haired girl answers, with "What's up sailor chief?"

Our FOB has multiple branches of the military, and I know under normal circumstances this informal greeting would be grounds for chastisement- but I'm on the hunt for a member of my team, and could care less how this girl answers- as long as she does.

"You know, Ryan, down in 10E?"

"Yeah, I know her. Hardly see her though."

"Did you see her yesterday at all?"

"Yessir. Just as I came back from dinner she was on her way out."

"How was she dressed."

It came out as an order and not a question.

She takes note of my serious tone and gives me the straightforward on my level, "Shorts, T-shirt, running shoes."

"Did she talk to you?"

"Just a hello, sir."

I turn on my heel and stride out of the barracks.

Hitting the sand I pause and try to imagine the path that Ryan would take to get a little exercise.

I turn to my left. She probably just twisted her ankle and is now at the Med tent icing it down. I should just check there first. Let Butters and Hanzo know what's going on too, so they can keep their eyes peeled just in case I miss her as she heads back to her bunk.

But...this scenario doesn't sit right with me. It doesn't take twelve plus hours to get a sprained ankle looked at and iced down.

I trust my gut. Instead of following the path I think Ryan might have taken, I take a right and head to operations command.

Pulling open the door, I take in the multiple TV screens, computer equipment, phones, and other paraphernalia crammed in the space haphazardly on desks.

A few fans stir the air, and in addition to Lieutenant Gervais, Captain Peters, and Rear Admiral Smith, there's four supporting personnel typing and talking on the phones.

Captain Peters addresses me first.

"Ah. Chief Broussard. We got your report yesterday. Good to know Seal Team Four is ready for duty."

"Sir. I have an issue - I need to review the security cameras from last night in sector four."

"Sector four? That's the residential sector."

"Yes sir." I try to keep the annoyance out of my voice.

"Broussard!" comes a command from Smith.

I make my way over to him. After our salute he begins, "James...Where is the SOCOM orders that came through yesterday?"

One of the newbies fresh out of boot camp brings a file over to the Admiral with a skittish eye flicked to me.

"Yes. Thank you, James."

James scuttles back behind a desk a good distance from us, while the admiral studies the paper he has pulled from the file.

"Specialized Details for executing order 1057B."

He hands me the paper. As I scan over it, he continues, "Joint research mission between SOCOM and CIA. We're testing the mettle of your one and only female team member."

I read the directive with uneasiness churning in my gut. It basically outlines and gives the authorization to execute a snatch and grab on Ryan for the purposes of an experimental interrogation to see how a female reacts to different interrogation tactics - not to last longer then a period of forty-eight hours. Fucking slithering CIA.

"Sir. You have got to be kidding me- we could be deployed at any minute on a highly volatile situation where we must be at 110%; we hardly need to be served up to the CIA for experimental interrogations. We have no way of knowing if what they are doing could have short term repercussions or long term complications. It's a severe and detrimental risk to put a team member through such a thing."

Not that we haven't been studied before- the effects of stress related combat on the body and such things. But this. This stank worse than a rotting whale carcass on a hot summer day.

"Broussard. I know this. But, we also need to know if training females for spec ops combat is a waste of time and money- if she cracks under the first sign of pressure - it's all for naught."

"I highly disagree. Sir. You are putting my team's lives on the line in an active combat deployment so the CIA can get their kicks in. We don't even know what condition Ryan will be in when they are done or even what interrogation tactics they are using on her."

71

He grunts in response and pulls a laptop across the desk towards us. He types in his pass code, and double clicks on a desktop camera icon.

A video stream fills the screen. Dim lighting makes it hard to see exactly, but a female form is restrained in the middle of the screen, laying down on a table, with a cloth over her face.

A man with a heavy beard and traditional Middle Eastern garb stands over her with a pitcher of water, while another form is standing at her head. They're shouting questions at her in Arabic, but she's not answering, just breathing hard.

They are fucking waterboarding her. As I watch they began pouring the water from the pitcher over her face as she thrashes on the table. I start to see red. C- Fucking - IA. They think their shit doesn't stink, and here they are imitating the enemy to try and break a soldier.

The water in the pitcher finally runs out, but Ryan keeps struggling and coughing. They switch to English, "Tell us little pussy, where are the American soldiers scouting next."

Ryan's cough starts to turn into laugh, and in the next few seconds she is outright chortling.

The "Arab" slams her head back against the table, and begins pouring water on her face again.

I slam the laptop closed and meet the Admiral's eyes.

"Sir. For the safety of my team, I ask that you release Ryan from this experiment ASAP. It's a liability for her to be in there." I can barely get the words past my lips my jaw is clenched so tight.

"Broussard. Calm Down. She's fine. The waterboarding is the worst of it. She'll be isolated in an hour, and then they are going to give her TS-199. After that, she'll be questioned a final time and released- no harm."

TS-199 is code for an interrogational truth serum. Highly hallucinogenic, interrogators have been using it for a while now to get information.

"Sir, I have to object."

"Duly noted. Broussard."

He gives me a glare and raised eyebrow. Flipping the paperwork back into the folder with finality he says, "You are dismissed...unless you have further business?"

I stare at his ambivalent eyes and picture punching him in the face and breaking his arrogant nose. It calms me a minute.

"No sir."

I'll have to figure out some other way to get Ryan out of this. It's all I can do to contain the rage at seeing her on that table. The only easy day was yesterday.

Before I can even close the door to operations all the way, I spot T-Rex hanging outside the door.

"Sir."

He falls in behind me as I fast walk back to Ryan's bunk.

"Sir. Can you tell me where's Ryan?"

I ignore him the whole time we walk.

"T..." I pause only when I am once again at the door to the girl's barracks.

"T," I begin again and look him directly in the eye, "The CIA grabbed her yesterday for an authorized interrogation. Joint direct orders from SOCOM."

His look of worried bewilderment slowly dissipates into anger.

"Bull-fucking-shit, Master Chief. We know those CIA motherfuckers don't do anything clean. And they have Ryan!?!?!"

"It's not good T," I pause wondering if I should share what I saw, "They got her for a full forty-eight hours and we are only sixteen in."

"FUCK!" He punches the wall of the barracks and leaves a T-Rex fist-sized dent in the siding.

Before he can rear back and do it again. I holler his name, "T!" and grab his arm.

He's breathing heavily but concentrates on me.

"I've got a plan. But I need you to go down to the CIA section and see if you can find out where they are holding her and who is charge in their camp."

He nods once and jogs off without a backward glance at me.

I pull open the girl's barracks door for a second time today. I don't announce myself this time, instead just make my way to Ryan's door.

Entering her room, I pull open her foot locker and lift out her laptop. It's 10:35AM here. San Diego is ten hours behind. So it should be around midnight there. Not ideal, but I hate to leave Ryan in the hands of those CIA fuckers another minute.

I power up her laptop, and open Skype. I scroll through her numbers and note that there's no men's names on the list. Just her sisters and father. I jot down the number to "Home and Dad Cell."

Double check that I wrote the numbers down correctly, then power the laptop back down and place it back in her locker.

I realize suddenly that we have left a member of our team alone for too long a time, vulnerable and unprotected. I'm disgusted with my oversight. Ryan's going to have to come live in with the rest of the team.

17

Ryan

Waking up strapped down to a rough wooden table, it's a feeling of helplessness so sharp and worrisome, for a minute panic overwhelms me.

I force myself to take three deep breaths and assess my situation.

My face is completely covered by a rough cloth, but dim light seeps around the edges enough to tell me where ever I am at, there's light. My hands are bound and stretched above my head. My feet and knees are also bound. No shoes, and I've lost my t-shirt. I've got a splitting headache and dry mouth.

"Good morning little American whore." A smooth voice speaks next to my right ear.

"You know how this goes, yes?"

I don't say anything but instead focus my senses outward, trying to determine if anyone else is in the room.

I hear a faucet turn on and water filling a bucket.

"Your name and rank, now little twat."

His accent is slightly off, not a hundred percent Arabic...but I am not sure what else I am hearing. And his use of the word twat is comical.

SHERRY L. BROWN

The water pouring over my face stuns me at first -it's abruptness paralyzing. It seems within seconds I'm unable to breathe and start struggling.

Just as abruptly as it started, it stops.

I gag and cough and try to catch my breath.

Again and again he asks me questions and pours water over my face.

I retreat to the portion of my brain where I'm unreachable and numb.

As if from a distance, my brain confirms the unbelievable for me. I'm being fucking water boarded. Again the water over my face, and myself choking and coughing, unable to breathe. I lose track of time, the interrogators questions seem endless. After a while, I do the really awesome, kickass, SEAL thing and pass out.

18

When I come too this time, I'm still blindfolded but sitting in a chair, arms bound behind me, feet tied beneath me. When I lift my head, my neck protests with a sharp ache so I know I've been in the position a while.

"Ahh. Little kitten. Are you prepared to answer any more of my questions?"

I tilt my head back trying to see under the blindfold, but all I can make out is a dirt floor, and a pair of boots in front of me- khaki pants tucked into them.

A sharp slap across my face whips my head to the left. I taste blood on the inside of my cheek.

"Now, BITCH. Tell me your name and rank!"

I give a short laugh, a huff really. He grips my chin and tilts my head up as if he could see my eyes behind the blindfold. I see the buttons on his dark green shirt. Smell his garlic breath.

"Don't speak up, and I'll make it permanent by cutting out your tongue. Then I'll feed it to dogs and leave you to rot in a dark hole."

"Do your worst," I tell him. Then tell myself, Good job, Ryan. Piss off the interrogator.

He thrusts my head back, cruelly. The force rocks my chair back.

I hear him walk a few feet away from me, and his voice carries across the room.

"I have something for you...It's a little cocktail to loosen that pretty tongue of yours."

His footsteps on the hard packed earth bring him back to my side, his presence discernable by the shift in light behind my blindfold. A sharp prick in my arm. Great. Who knows what drugs this guy just gave me.

"I'll be back in twenty minutes...enough time to let that stir your blood and improve your mood," he hisses at me in a low tone.

The minute he closes the door, I'm pulling my wrists at my back, trying to find any give in the bindings.

It's solid. My feet are on the ground, but my legs are tied to the chair. Thrusting up on my toes, I'm able to rock forward a bit. I put my complete body weight behind the movement, but none of the bindings give. A clammy sweat is breaking out between my breasts, and my feet are feeling tingly. I rock forward one more time, and my momentum carries me too far over. I crash hard forward- landing on my left shoulder and the side of my face.

I taste the dusty dirt and spit - reassessing my new predicament.

Sore left shoulder and cheek stinging with pain; Feet still tingling, and now hands too.

I've ended up on my side but still attached to the chair. I've dislodged my blindfold a bit though, and I take a minute to let my eyes move around the room. It's typical concrete walls, rough and dingy. Dim lighting provided by a couple of bulbs screwed directly into outlets high up in the wall. One table, metal. I can only see the legs from my vantage on the floor. One door, probably metal. That's it.

My vision blurs and I see eight table legs where before there were four. I take a deep inhale. It's the drugs. It's got my vision spinning.

I keep pulling at my wrists- despite the pain of the abrasions I'm most certainly creating in my struggles.

I alternately watch the door (behind me) and the tops of my thighs. I'm not getting anywhere with the ropes so I try to scoot to the table in front of me - in hopes that on top of it, there might be something on it that I can knock off and help myself with. How long has it been? Three minutes? Five?

I haven't been keeping track. I've managed to caterpillar to the leg of the table closest to me. Giving it a bump, when the sound of raised voices beyond the door freezes me before I can do it again. I'm straining to hear, when I see the snake. It's just beyond the opposite leg of the table, coiled up in an aggressive stance, hissing. It's about as long as my arm, black with shiny scales.

The panic has adrenaline flooding my system. Reflexively, I shoot backward in my hobbled state, and the snake follows in an attack lunge, plunging into my thigh.

FUCK. FUCK. The pain is sharp, almost cramp like, and I sob with the realization that I'll most likely die in this shit hole, not by gunshot, or IED, but from big ugly motherfuckin' snake.

I whimper, and try to dislodge it, but its whole jaw is working its way around my thigh. It's trying to swallow me whole.

I'm disgusted and panicked, thrusting my body in crazy motions, restricted and unable to dislodge the snake from its grip on my thigh.

Suddenly, I hear the door behind me open. I'd completely forgotten about it in my panic. Hopelessness sinks in my gut.

"RYAN! Ryan, can you hear me?"

Suddenly Chief Broussard's face appears over my right shoulder.

"Watch the snake, the motherfuckin' snake!" I yell at him.

It's dislodged itself from my thigh, but now lays coiled in front of us. Broussard follows my gaze, but his eyes move past it and keep scanning.

"Where's the snake, Ryan?" He cuts the bindings at my wrists as he asks.

"It's right there! Jesus, get us the fuck away from it!"

He's not pulling me backwards or moving fast enough, so I start working at the bindings on my knees, not looking at the puncture wounds on my thigh. Broussard has my feet free with just a slice of his knife, and the minute I feel the pressure of the ties go, I'm jumping up and backwards away from the snake, which now has it's mouth open, it's head wagging back and forth. As I watch it, transfixed, a hundred little snakes are birthed from its open mouth in an horrendous spewing. They are fast fuckers, inky black and coming for me and Broussard's feet.

He's not even looking at them. "Jesus, Fuck, BROUSSARD! SHOOT THE FUCKING THINGS!"

I'm jumping to the side, dancing to the left and right, but they are so fast they are on my feet and starting to slither up my shins. I don't know what to do. I'm swiping and jumping, swiping and jumping in a furious pace, when suddenly everything goes upside down, and I understand when I see Broussard's feet beneath me that he's thrown me over his shoulder. He's walking towards the door, though, not running and the snakes are still slithering around the floor, his boots, up the back of his legs.

"RUN! Broussard! RUN!" But he's doing nothing more than a fast walk.

"Calm down, Ryan. I've got you, just calm down." I hardly register his words. The snakes are up the backs of his thighs. I grab the service pistol at his hip and start firing into the writhing mass at his feet. Broussard drops me fast, I land hard on my butt, the clip empty, but the snakes are still there, larger now, as long as my leg. Before I can get up Broussard snatches the pistol from my hand and gets directly in my line of sight, grabbing both sides of my face to keep me immobile.

"The snakes, Broussard...." I feel the tears spilling down my cheeks. I've been poisoned and failed to protect Broussard. And now, now we were both certain to be dead or eaten alive by the ugly nasty snakes.

"LOOK. AT. ME. RYAN."

His command stops my eyes from scanning the sides of the hallway looking for the snake threat that he turned his back on.

"The snakes are a hallucination. There are no snakes."

It takes me a minute to understand what he's saying. He repeats it. Takes my hand and helps me up. He moves out of my straight line of vision down the hallway, and there it is, the biggest snake I've ever seen in my life, coming straight for us.

I back up, but Broussard grabs my hand and holds me in place. The urge to run is overwhelming. My muscles quake in anticipation.

"...Broussard...Please..." I whisper.

He must understand my request, because he wraps his arm around my shoulder and leads me the opposite way down the hall, and out a door.

The light is gold-blue, letting me know it's either sunset or sunrise. My heartbeat is erratic and pumping hard in my chest. I am panting, my throat raw, unable to focus on the figures around me. Broussard pushes me into sitting, and there is Hanzo.

He places a scratchy wool blanket around my shoulders and I clutch it to my chest.

He puts a pen light up to my eyes, which I quickly knock away. Hanzo's eyes narrow in exasperation, and he turns to Broussard beside me. Broussard grabs my wrist and holds it to my side, so that the next time Hanzo lifts the light to my eyes, I am unable to knock it away.

Satisfied, he tucks the light in a pocket and starts probing my face with his hands. His thumb hits the tender spot high on my left cheekbone and I hiss in pain and pull backwards- directly against Broussard's chest.

"Settle down, Ryan. The faster you cooperate, the faster this will be over with."

His hands are on the outside of my upper arms.

"The snake, Hanzo. Check my leg. Check my leg. The snake bit me." I'm speaking fast and panicked but I don't care.

Hanzo has already moved on to fastening the blood pressure cuff to my arm. He's ignoring me while methodically getting my vitals. I pull forward this time, but again Broussard has me and pulls me back against his chest, restraining me so Hanzo can complete his tests.

"Hanzo, please...Please just check."

He looks down at my legs and then back up at me.

"Your clean, Ryan. No bite marks, You're good." His eyes trail over my shoulder.

"I'm going to give her a mild sedative, Chief; Her vitals are off the charts. Too much more and we'll have a heart attack on our hands." My whole body is tense, I start fighting Broussard's hold. No way am I letting them shoot me with anything else. It's such a short time to have been drugged twice and poisoned by a snake, it's no wonder my vitals are off the charts- I'm a walking cocktail. I struggle while trying to explain to Hanzo, but my words are jumbled, not making sense even to my own ears and, Broussard has me solidly immobilized.

Without preamble, Hanzo has the needle up to my bicep and the plunger down.

He steps back while Broussard loosens his grip. His mistake. I launch myself out of his arms, and knock Hanzo down with my forward momentum, my already sore shoulder painfully connecting with his chest. He sprawls in the dirt, but I don't stop. Two long strides, three, when I am tripped up by my own feet and take a very ungraceful nosedive in the dirt, my palms, elbows and knees catching me painfully.

I roll off my stomach and stare up a moment into the dark blue sky, a few stars twinkling at me. My breathing is slowing down a bit. Broussard's face breaks into my field of vision, but I can't make out the details in shadow.

He questions, "You done?"

I take stock. While my stomach still feels in turmoil, my heartbeat is not bursting out of my chest any longer, and my arms and legs feel like lead weights instead of electrified coils.

I nod my head, and he holds his hand out to pull me up, but when I'm vertical my legs crumple beneath me. Broussard doesn't hesitate to take all my weight and then sweep me up into his arms.

As he walks, I process what I am seeing and hearing now that the panic has worn off. Two men's voices raised in argument, the tops of the plywood buildings that make up the FOB passing by in my field of vision.

"Good of you to call in the higher-ups on this one, Broussard; What's your problem anyway, can't let your cat out to play?"

I turn my head towards the taunter. Khaki pants, tucked into brown boots. Green shirt and a good enough looking face, I suppose. But I know immediately who this is by the weird accent tinting his words and the hate bubbles up in my gut.

Broussard must have felt the shift in my demeanor, because he turns and places me back on the seat of a golf cart, so my back is to this man. I hear T-Rex's voice break in, "Shut the fuck up, Garner. Stay the fuck away from Ryan, and sure as fuck away from us. Next time we meet, I might not be so nice."

I hear a scuffle, like a boot scraping dirt, but don't turn around. Broussard is climbing into the driver's seat of the cart. "Yo! T! Let's go!"

As we drive, Hanzo is questioning where I hurt, how many times I've lost consciousness, questioning my hallucinations, all the while probing my head, my shoulder, rinsing the dirt from my hands and making me rotate my limbs in various exercises.

"Petty Officer Ryan, do you need to visit the medical tent?" He ends his line of questioning.

"Ugh. No." I rub my forehead; my brain is trying to process, but it's like I'm swimming in bowl of sticky syrup trying to add the facts ups.

I am Everly Ryan. Petty Officer, 2nd class, US Navy. Deployed to FOB in Syria. I was kidnapped and interrogated. I was hallucinating ugly, disgusting, snakes. I was hallucinating. I am hallucinating. Maybe I'm still back there. Tied to that chair giving up all the secrets of my life, my team, the military to the enemy....

"T-Rex. T-Rex! Tell me something true."

"Shit Ry. You just got water boarded by the CIA- but I'm proud of you girl- still came out swinging. What you want me to say?"

He gives me a lopsided grin, and it's one I know so well. I lean forward in my seat and grip his cheeks. It feels real.

He pats my hands awkwardly and I drop them back to my lap.
"You're good Ry. Broussie here pulled some strings and got you out."

I look at Broussard. He's resolute, all business as he pulls in front of the guy's clubhouse and comes around to pull me from my seat.

I'm shivering in the cold desert night air. Standing on my feet feels like I'm ninety years old with creaking bones. T- Rex holds the clubhouse door open, and I slowly climb the three steps to get up and through the threshold. I know Broussard is just behind me, ready to catch me should I fall. It's annoying enough to have me pushing forward under my own steam.

The lights are low, there's only Butters sitting in front of the flat screen, with Hanzo, T-Rex and Broussard coming in behind me.

Butters salutes me with an Xbox controller, "Yo! Ryan. Nice Shiner. You give them CIA boys hell?"

I just nod once and look for a soft spot to crash. The clubhouse is my nickname for the common space the boys are assigned with their individual "bunks" (cubicle like rooms) on two sides of the building.

Hanzo walks to his own bunk, complete with plywood door, with a smile and some medical advice of "get some rest and drink plenty of water."

Broussard brushes past me with a gruff, "Follow me, we've got you set up in here, Ryan."

Before I can follow though, T-Rex engulfs me in a bear hug that cuts off my air supply.

"Jesus, Fuck- T! Give her some fucking space!" This from an impatient Broussard waiting at a far cubby across the room.

I make my way over to him and peek in. It's utilitarian, but I notice my foot locker and Red Sox cap occupying the space.

'It's yours Ryan. Right here with the team."

I nod once and sit wearily down on the bunk closing my eyes.

"Thanks Chief."

The door claps shut loudly. But I'm surprised when I hear the whisper of fabric as Broussard's body moves towards to me. I open my eyes and tilt my head to look up at him.

He cups both his hands around my face.

"Listen Ryan. I'm the bunk next door. You need anything - you just say my name, and I'll be here."
I just give him a circumspect nod in the affirmative. But he doesn't move away immediately and keeps his warm palms cupping the sides of my face. His eyes are roving over my face, and he pauses at my left cheek and runs his thumb across it.

"I'll get you some ice."

I break out into goose bumps. Whether it is from the caress or the thought of ice I don't know.

His eyes continue to run down my body to my breasts and up to my shoulder that is throbbing painfully. He takes one step backwards, breaking the intimacy of the moment.

"Lots of ice...And something to eat and drink. Any special requests?"

I shake my head. Lifting my arms up to pull my sports bra over my head, Broussard spins quickly on his heel and bangs out the door.

I peel my panties and shorts down my legs together in one swoop. I feel immeasurably vulnerable standing there naked in a space that is not my own. I pull a fresh pair of my favorite boy short panties from my locker, as well as a black tank top that I quickly pull down over my chest.

I sit back down on the bed and take stock. I'm tired and dirty.

I climb beneath the covers, too exhausted to care about the dirt, to emotionally drained to care about what happened. I seek escape and sleep is it.

19

Broussard

Closing the door quickly on Ryan's almost naked form, I take a deep breath. She's ok. Safe. I travel over to our camp stove and food storage. Rummage through the panels and find a lasagna MRE. It's the most comforting food I can seem to find. It'll have to do. I leave it to heat up while I locate a snap cold pack and a couple bottles of water.

I gather up all the items and bring them back to Ryan's bunk. Pushing open the door, I find her laid out, under the covers, eyes closed. Her cheek is bruising nicely, her lower lip on the right side swollen and her shoulder is turning a really nice shade of grape-like purple.

I place the items on the foot locker next to her head and shake her awake.

She reluctantly opens her eyes.

"Are you hungry, Ryan?"

She sits up and the blanket falls to her lap.

Her breasts are free and pressing against the confines of her tank top. Her nipples hard and noticeable. I look away and pull the fork from my pocket and hand her both the lasagna and fork.

She dutifully takes a couple bites, but when she spots the water bottle, she unscrews the lid and chugs damn near the whole thing.

Putting the empty bottle, the half-eaten lasagna on the locker next to her head, she lays back down without much of an acknowledgement to me.
I hand her the ice pack, but instead of putting it on her face, she places it on her shoulder. Guess I know what hurts the most.

"Thanks, Chief." Her eyes close. And just like that I am dismissed.
I take the discarded dinner with me and shut the door behind me.

Hanzo is standing in the common area.

"She'll be ok, Chief."

"Yea, Hanzo. She's good."

He turns off the main lights, and now the space is dimly lit. I retire to my own bunk, pulling my belt off, the attached holster, and check my piece one last time. It's empty. I'll have to get more ammo tomorrow. Not sure if any repercussions will come from Ryan discharging all the rounds into the CIA's floor.

As I lay down in my boxers and t-shirt, I let the weight of worry fall off me. I got Ryan back. She's tucked safely next to me, our bunks aligned head to head, so really there is only thin plywood separating us. I take a deep breath. Yea. I got Ryan back, and the relief is so deep, I fall asleep the minute I shut my eyes.

20

Something has woken me. I lay for a minute in the darkness wondering what it could be. Then I hear it again. A strange clacking. Its different from the usual snores I hear when sharing space with the men. Different enough to have brought me out of a deep sleep. I strain to hear anything else. There it is again. What is it?

My brain finally connects the dots. It's Ryan next door shivering. I get out of bed and grab the fleece pullover from my locker that I keep for cold nights.

Quietly easing into Ryan's bunk, I lift a battery-operated lantern high with one hand and use my other to pull the ice pack from her shoulder.

She comes awake, and I signal for her to sit all the way up.

I pull the fleece over her head and tuck it down to her hips, ignoring the silkiness of her skin and the sexy tousled and sleepy look she is giving me. I'm seeing her now. I'm feeling her. And she is all warm woman.

I hastily pull up the blanket to her chin when she doesn't do it fast enough.

I reach back for the lantern and her hand shoots out and stops me.

"Broussard, thank you."

She closes her eyes and I know, I am again dismissed.

This time when I hit my bunk again, the images of a sexy sleep tousled Ryan replays on the back of my eyelids, and soon I'm imagining a different scenario, where instead of covering her up, I'm uncovering her, palming her warm breasts, feeling that silky skin heat up with my lips.

I give a small groan at the erection now in my shorts. It's not right, I know. But something about Ryan- I can't figure it out- I just am attracted to it.

I roll over and punch my pillow beneath my head. I've been separated from Miranda for more than eight months and had not felt the tiniest twinge in my libido. Now, here in the middle of the night, in the middle of an FOB, Mr. Happy is waking up. And he's taken notice of a five-ten brunette under my command. Fuck.

It's just that she's forbidden fruit- being under my command. I feel extremely protective of her. And she's hot dammit. Long lean legs, round breasts, and face to launch a thousand ships as they say.

I palm my erection one last time.

21

Ryan

I slowly peel my eyes open, and groan at the pain that shoots through my body when I try to roll over. I take stock after I'm on my side, and see the plain and rough plywood looks different from my normal plain rough plywood. I groggily stand up and contemplate the fleece I'm wearing. Dipping my nose into the collar, I inhale its scent- clean and masculine. I remember freezing last night, but unwilling to get up - then Broussard coming in and dropping his fleece over my head. I pull on my shorts and try not to backtrack too far down yesterday's memories.

Pulling open the door, I'm greeted by the brightness of a new day. I wish I could hit the dimmer switch because the light is piercing to my headache.

I don't even acknowledge the two guys sitting on the couch- just shuffle over to the kitchen area and make myself a cup of coffee from the Keurig- funny the amenities we have out here.

I plunk my butt down in one of the rolling chairs that sits permanently in front of the Xbox and close my eyes, leaning my head back.

"All right, Ryan?" the voice comes just to the right of me. I think it's Hanzo.

"...yeah. I'm fine."

And I am. I take stock. Shut down the anger, the fear at being unable to control my situation.

Take a sip of this crap coffee- no cream or sugar. Even though I love a little vanilla flavored creamer and spoonful of sugar, I gave up those frou-frou girly amenities when I entered the military.

"Good. You can help me beat Hendricks here."

An X-Box control hits my arm and I grab it with one hand while leaning over to place my coffee cup on the floor with the other hand.

I don't argue; just take my frustrations out on a little video game action. It's *Call of Duty* and I happen to play like a girl.

Broussard saves me from making a total fool of myself though, by coming in from outside twenty minutes later. He interrupts our game by tapping me on the shoulder with a sat phone.

"Ryan. Glad your up. The Admiral has been waiting to hear from you."

My stomach drops. I look up at Broussard while taking the phone in my hand.

Broussard's eyes are boring into mine with a look I can't read.

"He said he'd only be satisfied when he heard from you directly."

My stomach drops as I stand up and hand the controller back to Hanzo.

I turn to Broussard fully while the guys go back to electronic numbness.

"What do you mean? My father?" I question the admiral he's referring to.

Broussard reaches out and holds my elbow steering me a little further away from the video game onslaught.

"Listen, Ryan. When you…" He pauses and takes a deep breath and places his thumb and forefinger at the bridge of his nose.

"When I found out the CIA had you- those orders were direct from SOCOM."

My brain begins churning a million different thoughts. I feel betrayed by my own country in a way. I mean I kind of knew it had to be an inside job, but now I fully make all the connections- thank you brain-focusing caffeine. Emotions are churning in my head, but the top one is a shame that my commander pulled strings by calling my "Daddy" to get me out of situation that I should have -not just survived but thrived- under.

"What the fuck, Broussard?"

The understanding in eyes tells me he didn't like it anymore then I did. His at first soft look switches in an instant to his pissed off commander stare.

"Just call your father and tell him you're ok, Ryan. That's an order."

He spins on his heels and bangs out the door. I dial Dad on the SAT and take a deep breath while it rings.

"Everly? You ok?"

"Not even a hello, Dad?"

"Broussard tells me you got a little banged up, but just superficial bruises."

Jesus. Broussard and my father discussing me. It does weird things to my chest to think he cared enough to tell my father how I was.

"It's nothing, Dad."

That's all he is getting. I would not elaborate in case he thinks this is the reason he should enforce the part of our agreement that said I would leave the SEALs if I got injured.

"Ok, Everly. Make sure you watch your six. And make sure you follow Broussard's orders. He's one of the best SEALs I know."

"Yes sir."

I hang up without much else. I am oddly bereft that Broussard and my father seem to have some type of relationship. Had they met before? Or had they forged a connection in what I could only think had to be a couple phone calls.

I couldn't seem to get anything other than hate stares from Broussard- and here's my dad all chummy with him.

Broussard

When a woman wears your clothes, it's a base sign that she belongs to you. In the middle of the night, the significance of putting the sweater on Ryan was lost on me. But in the light of day, she's still wearing it, and like a punch to the gut I want to pull her in my arms and declare her mine. It's fucking disgusting how much I want this warrior woman. I've seen her come alive on training missions, go all in with no holes barred- and I've admired it. But a vulnerable, soft Ryan? It stirs my instincts and has me going all cave-man, thinking I can lay claim to her as a man.

I hit the weights hard, pushing myself to fatigue and forget about how silky and warm her skin is at night.

22

Ryan

A week and half later and I get my first DA or direct
assault. Nothing too treacherous as the Chief debriefs us.
It's an assist evacuation of a communal home that is being
used as a combo women's shelter/orphanage. We load up
in the Humvees and crawl through town - convoy style. I'm
on point to help calm the situation as a female presence.
That's exactly how the Chief phrased it, "Female presence."
I don't take offense, a mission is a mission. One of the
interpreters is female too.

The building is a Frankenstein mishmash of
townhouse like proportions. Clearing the first floor is
relatively easy; we load up two single moms with five
children between them easy peasy into the transport van.
Moving to the second story, we clear two other families
with only minimal fuss. I've moved on to the second to last
family that's being transported, where Sanja the interpreter
with the government facilitator explaining the situation.

There seems to be some discussion/argument over
where they are going and what has been promised to them
when they get there. After five minutes- in which during
I've been subtly sweeping the living room- the situation

seems to be escalating instead of diffusing. The baby in the back room begins to wail louder than a banshee.

Chief Broussard steps past the women in the living room arguing and heads towards me.

"Grab the baby, Ryan. See if you can get it calmed down while I try to hurry this train along."

I roll my eyes at the command, knowing he probably only did it because I'm a woman. I just give him a, "Yes sir."

I spin on the hand woven rug and enter the backroom. It's really the size of a walk-in closet, but at the far wall, a baby blue crib, its color a bright splash against the white wall. The baby has kicked off the blanket, it's cotton softness is spilling out the crib slats and trailing on the floor.

I do a quick scan, but nothing more as I hustle over to the crib - feeling the urgency to get to the baby and quiet it down making me move fast. I only realize something is wrong when my right boot heel lands on something...different from the rest of the floor. It's enough to make me pause. Feel the sweat trickle down my breasts.

I take a deep breath.

"Sshh...little baby..."

He hesitates mid-cry when he sees me. Dark hair, red round face still scrunched up, deciding if he should continue to cry. No need to panic yet. Right?

I lightly speak into my com, "Chief, need your assistance ASAP."

I keep my tone light, but hope he doesn't take too long.

A few moments pass and I keep up a stream of nonsensical words to keep the baby quiet. He's -while not happy- curious enough about me to be entertained.

I soon hear steps behind me.

"Chief." I put my hand up behind me in a stop signal and look over my shoulder.

He immediately halts inside the door.

"Step lightly, sir. Need you to take this baby."

"Ryan? Why can't you just bring the baby out?"

"...sir..." I don't really know how to finish the sentence.

He's soon behind me without any sound.

"Shit! Not so close!"

I don't want him to go if for some reason reaching in for the baby detonates this thing. For all I know it could be pressure sensitive or time...limit casualties is what I've got to do.

In my peripheral vision I see him take a step back.

I take a deep breath and reach into the crib hooking the baby under the armpits. Freaking thing is heavier than a sack of potatoes.

I don't even take the chance of cradling him to me to offer comfort, I just twist my upper body back, arms outstretched with the baby.

Broussard takes him and gives him the comfort I couldn't. His eyes shine green and full of concern, in the glimpse I get before turning back forward.

"Stay sharp, Ryan. Calling in EOD now."

I take a deep breath and start to count; its a relaxation and calming method I use. I stare at the white plaster wall. Make the count to five hundred, notice a little nail hole that hasn't been filled back in. Time slows down to an excruciating crawl.

Finally EOD arrives as a fourth droplet of sweat glides down my back and absorbs into my waistband. They send in the mars rover- at least that's what I call their remote control robot. I can feel the crowd behind the door, tense, as the rover's little zzzrrts and zzzats move it this way and to investigate what's beneath my foot.

Broussard is in my ear over the com:

"All...right...Ryan...looks like we got a semi standard pressure bomb here."

A few seconds tick by that feel like hours. Every muscle in my body is tensed. As if I just spring off fast enough I could beat this thing. I give a deep sigh and try to relax my shoulders.

"Ryan. Lieutenant Jenkins is coming in. Standby."

The robot backs out and I feel a body come in behind me ever so softly; he kneels down beside my foot. I don't even move my head to look at what he is doing but I feel him softly brushing dirt away.

A few moments pass where I have completely zoned out.

"Ok, what we got here is a standard pressure bomb in the wall with line detonator under Ryan's foot here. Bring her a flak jacket. Ryan, we'll get that on you and then I'll cut the detonation line before we diffuse the bomb so that you can get out of here."

I risk moving my eyes down to where Jenkins is. He's older, round face, clear eyes behind his safety-goggles.

Fucking middle-aged softie. Probably has a pack of kids at home.

"No. Give me the cutters, and tell me which line to cut- I'll do it when you're clear."

"Ryan…" He looks down at where he has completely uncovered the wires leading to the wall.

"Don't argue with me on this. I'm already at risk…"

I'm interrupted by a voice over in my earpiece. "Ryan, let EOD do their fucking jobs." It's a weird echo, as Broussard's voice also carries from just beyond the door behind me.

"Excuse me, Master Chief. I have to respectfully disagree. I am doing it. We already know the score. Hand me the cutters, Jenkins, and show me where. Then clear the fucking area."

"Ryan, you don't have to prove you have the biggest balls." It's spoken so quietly over the line, so quietly I don't hear the echo from where he is speaking beyond the doorway.

There's really no comeback to that. I'm not trying to prove anything. I just know the score, and I'm not sacrificing middle-aged Jenkins, EOD expert and probably father of three.

"Jenkins," I say clearly, "the wire cutters, please." Jenkins shows me where to cut, I have to move my head to get a good look- but other then that I keep absolutely still. My glute is starting quiver.

"Jenkins clear!" comes a yell from beyond the doorway.

I bend slowly at my knees going straight down, not moving my footprint. The wire cutters are in my right hand, hovering over the exposed wires.

"Anytime Ryan." Comes Broussard's voice over the line.

"Give me a fucking second." I grind back at him. I'm just a little fucking tense right now. I try not to imagine being blasted into a thousand pieces.

The wire cutters are spring loaded, so I just slip the open nose over the wire Jenkins showed me. I squeeze my fist and the wire is cleanly cut. My stomach jumps in relief, but I know that's not all there is. I straighten and speak into the comm, "Wire cut. Stepping off now."

I lift my right boot straight off the ground and then behind me. Silence. I take a deep breath and calmly walk all the way back. At the doorway, there's a crowd with Jenkins at the front. He claps me on the shoulder. "Balls of steel, Ryan. Balls of steel." He turns back to his EOD team as they again are now setting up the rover to go in and retrieve and detonate the IED.

I smack his shoulder back. "Thanks man. I owe you a beer."

Broussard is right behind him- looking pissed off with barely contained rage, I see his jaw muscles tensing.

"Fall in, Ryan."

He gives me his back, and I follow out to our transport.

T-Rex is there and everyone can read that the Chief is not happy, so the ride back to base is pretty quiet. For my part, my brain can't comprehend that someone would put a bomb in a baby's room. Damn- that's some fucked up shit.

Broussard

I felt like my foot was on that bomb, not Ryan's. As I stare into her electric eyes, I can feel my arms aching to take hold of her and shake some damn sense into the stubborn brain of hers. Damn. She just couldn't let the bomb guys do their fucking jobs.

Feelings are bubbling in my gut- anger, pride, and overwhelming joy. How could she not follow my orders? I hate it, am miffed that she would so willingly risk her life, and step up to the plate to save others. I'd seen glimpses of her depths before, her commitment to the team, but never to this length. All of my emotions are threatening to come out of my throat and make a fool of myself in front of everyone.

I stomp them down hard. Compartmentalize.

23

Ryan

The Middle East is the freaking dustiest place on earth. It's been three and half months of hot boring time. Mostly, we do a lot of security escorts and patrols and waiting around for orders. So when a joint task force meeting is called, I'm excited for the potential for something different. Sitting in the "classroom" listening to our XO and the other SOCOM commanders brief us on the mission, our targets and intel reconnaissance, I'm perfectly focused. There's nothing to distract, being in a room with no windows and only various information posted on the walls.

T-Rex is beside me, making notes in his notebook; his own focus intense. The room is filled with other spec ops personnel and officers- everyone involved in this DA. We'll be attempting to take over a large square block of buildings that the jihadist have been using as a temporary base of sorts. While the Air Force will target the main five story structure on one side, we are to secure the street behind it working with a team of Marines to clear the buildings. Fun stuff.

After an hour of intense information, we are released to get ready. I stand up, and head to the exit at the back of

the room behind my team. Passing by the few men still
lingering -a sudden hand grabs my right ass cheek.

Instinct kicks in and I've got that hand in my grip,
spun the body it was attached to in front of me and
slammed the offender's face into the closest wall nice and
easy like.

It's some asshole pilot that made a comment at the
beginning of the briefing about feminists in combat. It
wasn't nice. I ignored it then, but now I realize he's a sexist
asshole with a chip on his shoulder.

I hate fuckers like this. I pull his hand up higher where
it is twisted behind his back. He squawks in response. I hear
scuffling behind me and know T has my back.

The culprit is panting against the wall- holding in
anymore exclamations of pain.

I lean in real close to his ear and whisper, "Keep your
hands to yourself flyboy, you understand?'"

He shuffles his feet and tries to push me off, make me
let go, but I have an excellent pin on him, and I just pull up
on his hand giving him a little more pain to let him know
who has the upper hand- literally. The quiet of the room
behind me alerts me to the fact that our little drama has
now commandeered center stage.

"RYAN! CROSS! Break it up!" comes a commanding
bark from somewhere over my shoulder.

I release the schmuck's arm and step back.

As expected, T is behind me, as well as Meaty and
Butters.

The schmuck is cradling his hand while a few of his
friends glare at me from beside him.

An Air Force officer walks between our two parties,
his face the color of a tomato, with a vein pulsing in his
forehead.

"WHAT the FUCK is going on HERE?!!?!"

I keep my mouth shut and hope he realizes the scene
speaks for itself. One woman trained in combat, a roomful

of guys - one with a new (hopefully) broken wrist. Maybe things are a little bit cloudy for him, because he turns from Cross and gives me a glaring look.

"Broussard! Handle up on your team! I don't want to see their ugly faces until we are ready to lock and load." He barks the order without looking away from me.

Broussard walks from the front of the room, past our little group to the door and holds it open for us. His eyes are drilling me, but I keep my head up and my shoulders straight as we file out one by one with T-Rex leading the way.

Following T-Rex's back I count backwards from one hundred, hoping to chase my anger away. I can still feel that asshole's hand on my butt and I feel like I need ten gallons of germ-x and a two week scalding hot shower to get rid of the gross violated feeling.

"Ryan! Follow me!"

I can't ignore the direct order, so I just keep counting as I follow Broussard's back to a small side office, where he closes the door behind us.

He takes up his standard arms-crossed-over-chest stance in front of me- eyes studying my face in trepidation. I can't really read how mad he is- but his wide legged stance and crossed arms give me a pretty good idea.

"Tell me, Ryan. What the fuck was that?"

How to put this without further pissing him off? I guess he hadn't seen the butt-grab.

Before I can began, he's already launched into his next sentence.

"You're supposed to be on your best god-damn behavior. You are representing the team and more importantly, me, in briefings like that. And you can't fucking play nice?"

"Sir. If I may?"

The look on his face says I should probably just shut up.

I do.

"Your pulling graveyard guard duty for the next two weeks, Ryan."

Guard duty was the suckiest assignment. Sitting above one of the gate entrances to the FOB, and we usually rotated graveyard shift. Looks like I was the lucky one.

"Anything to say for yourself? No? Good. Your lucky I don't pull you off this op."

"Yes. Sir."

"You're dismissed."

I escape the close confines of the office quickly. Trying to think of anything other than the pissed of commander I just left behind.

Fucking flyboy. Groped me and I was the one pulling guard duty for two weeks. I really hope I sprained his wrist good.

Broussard

No wonder women and men don't mix well in the military. What the fuck had Ryan been thinking? I follow her out of the office, but took a detour to the men's restroom before heading back to the briefing room our team was using. I am seeing red. Embarrassed that an Air Force Captain had to reprimand one of my team. And, let's be honest. Ryan already attracts enough scrutiny, I don't need her actions making further difficulties. Our team is under the fucking magnifying glass all the time, because she's one of us. I rinse my hands at the sink and pull a paper towel off the roll to dry my hands. T-Rex enters the head and takes a stance at the pisser.

He doesn't look at me, but says, "You know, Chief, that cocksucker grabbed her ass."

My stomach drops at his words. It makes total sense now why the scuffle happened. And Ryan's look of consternation when I wouldn't let her get a word in edgewise.

This is why I think to myself, I don't want a fucking girl on my team.

"Guess she handled it then." I tell T-Rex, even though I'm annoyed at myself.

I should have taken fifteen seconds and listened to her explanation. Then gone back in there and finished the job for her, given that asswipe a black eye and bloody nose. But, I'm hard on her. Because if I admit the truth to myself, I'm deeply attracted to her, and being hard on her, punishing her, not listening to what she has to say, it's my defense against that attraction.

Am I still hoping she'll give up and go home? Yes.

I stomp out of the head and to the supply room to gear up.

There is a mission to complete. I can worry about Ryan later.

24

Ryan

We hit the target early in the morning, hopefully before any tangos are awake. The sun is just coming up as our rolling convoy pulls into position. I don't really like clearing multiple story buildings, as it means we lose high-ground advantage. But, here I am, with six marines, and three of my team, T-Rex, Hanzo and of course our esteemed leader Broussard, silently climbing a stair well in the south corner of building two.

As we clear the west side, we hear gunfire erupt from the east. The building is a shelled out concrete apartment building. We hurriedly clear out the three east facing apartments while communicating to the other teams to find out what is going on.

The gunfire is coming from a building kitty corner to the one we are in. In less than thirty minutes the one behind us will be fodder for the Air Force's highly targeted missiles.

"Alpha Team needs cover," is the command consensus.

"Delta Team has a good visual," is the return confirmation.

"We are clear to engage," comes Broussard's yell from the corner apartment. I swear these buildings are put together with paper and spit, his voice comes through so clearly from two rooms away.

I look to Hanzo and he knocks out the glass from our east facing window.

Hanzo, a Marine named Sullivan, and I take positions.

I can just make out the shadowy figures on the ramparts of the building across the street. It's probably less than a hundred yards.

They are doing a good job of taking cover in between firing rounds at Alpha team.

I don't hesitate- just lay down some suppressive cover. The rat-tat-tat of my gun is not the only one echoing in my ear.

A bullet hits the concrete wall just beneath me.

I duck down to reload. "Yo, chief. Return Fire. Twelve o'clock."

I'm a bit in disbelief that it came from directly across from us. What'd they do, drop us down in an infested snake pit? The intelligence we had said those buildings were empty as of two hours before our targeting time- according to infrared imaging from a satellite.

"Confirmed. Tangos at twelve o'clock."

I look at Hanzo and Sullivan where they had taken cover next to me.

"Can you get a grenade over there, Hanzo?"

"Shit no. It's more likely to fall down into the street."

I was just about to ask for other options, when the whizz bang of grenade launcher registers in my brain.

I grab the marine next to me by the front of his shirt and pull him with me. I'm not sure if it is my forward momentum or a push from the grenade blast, but we clear the room entirely and land in a crumpled heap beneath plaster and concrete in the hall.

Pushing into a sitting position I check on Sullivan. He is laid out, but coughing dust - so I know he is breathing.

Before I can yell to Hanzo, Broussard is in my face, pulling me up by my Kevlar vest and yelling at me.

"ARE YOU OK? TALK TO ME RYAN."

"I'm fine…" I do a quick scan on my body. Bruises and my right ear seems to be throbbing painfully, but…"I'm fine."

"WE'RE FALLING BACK."

I nod my affirmative, while he turns around to give orders.

Just then an enormous boom shakes the entire building. It comes from the west side, the Air Force guys had found their target.

Hanzo is already up, with gun at the ready, looking hardly the worse for wear. Guess me and Sullivan had been in the main blow out area.

T-Rex pats me on the back as he passes, and a cloud of plaster dust puffs up from my shoulder. We go round the building and back down the stairs. I collect my nerves and stuff them away so I can be at the ready as we exit the building.

The only problem is, the gunfire from across the street has us pinned down and unable to get back to our convoy where it is parked to the south of us.

The first floor team, Charlie, already has good defensive positions and are laying out return fire. We stand just inside the doorway, catching our breaths while Broussard is on the comm requesting backup to hit the tangos from the back.

A couple more grenades hit the building, their deep booms echoing in the stairwell, but not causing any damage. The gunfire keeps up it's constant rat-tat-tat.

Broussard yells, "Backup denied. Airstrike Denied. We're going to split up and circle around. Delta team with me. Charlie team stay here and keep 'em occupied. Give me an ammo count!"

T-Rex yells a "Hoo-Yah! Four up!" Meaning he had four magazines left.

Hanzo, Sullivan and I all give our counts as we file in for a short walk.

Broussard

I scan the hall for Ryan. She is leaning against the wall-face dirty white with plaster dust and sweat. A little trickle of blood from her right ear, most likely a ruptured eardrum. I consider ordering her to stay hunkered down here with Charlie team, but immediately dismiss the idea when my gut protests at separating. The best way to look out for her, protect her, is to keep her close.

As T-Rex leads the team around to the back exit, I call out an order for Ryan on our comm line.

"Give me a report, Ryan. What's your status?"

"All good, Chief."

She gives me a thumbs up before bringing her rifle to her shoulder and ducking low and left out the back door.

I follow, laying out the route in my head, recalling the geographic maps and our positioning. It should take us less than fifteen minutes to circle the outside block and come up behind the tangos.

The first seven minutes go fine. It is when we go to cross an alley that all hell breaks lose. Zips and splats of gunfire erupts, hitting all around and in the alley; half the team has already crossed ahead of me and T-Rex. The last marine to cross was the unlucky one- bleeding from a gunshot wound in his leg, laying down in the middle of the alley. Before I can communicate our location, and ask for a med team, Ryan has breaks into the middle of the alley, Hanzo laying down cover fire for her while she drags the marine back behind the cover of the far building. I lay down my own cover fire for her, while acknowledging the sharp stab of panic that has my heartbeat increasing tempo the minute I see Ryan break into the alley. The fear and panic do crazy things to my chest and I don't like it.

She and Hanzo are now assessing the injuries, rapidly pulling things from his med kit, while the other members of the team stand protective and alert around them.

I am beyond tired of this FUBAR situation. I call in our location, and thankfully, the higher-ups gave the OK for a little more firepower relief in the form of a missile loaded Humvee. It makes short work of the insurgents in the alley, and we are able to get the marine medevac'd quickly. We continue our trek to circle around the block, and come up behind the tangos pinning Alpha team down.

Thankfully, the element of surprise is on our side, and we are able to quickly eliminate them. Some realize the futility of their situation within moments and after a twenty minute gun battle- give up.

We re-clear the buildings. I take note of the hole in the wall where Ryan was when I pass by it a second time. It is the size of a Volkswagen. The fear that I could have been mopping Ryan off these plaster walls is real. I don't know why it seems so much worse than the normal worry I feel for those under my command. I just know I don't like it one bit.

25

Ryan

Just another day in the desert. I'm rehashing some of the day's events as I sit outside the guard tower watching the gate below me. It's three-thirty AM and nothing is stirring.

"South Tower, standard check. No activity." I speak into my comm.

A few moments later, as I am stifling a yawn, the tower door opens, and out walks Chief Broussard.

"Hey, Ryan."

He sits down beside me and when I inhale, his clean masculine scent tickles my senses.

"Hey, Chief."

We are both quiet for a few moments. I'm trying to come up with some reason for him being out here, but all I can come up with is that he is checking up on me.

"You did good today, Ryan."

"Thanks, Chief."

Seconds tick by, minutes and nothing breaks the interlude.

"I wanted to apologize, Ryan," Chief Broussard begins, "I should have listened to your explanation about the scuffle in the briefing room yesterday morning."

I'm flabbergasted. I think this is the first time any commander of mine as apologized- and quite a turnaround from the usual annoyance I read from Broussard.

"Oh. Um…" is all I get out in response before hastily tacking on, "apology accepted."

We sit quietly for a few minutes more, and a chill breeze causes me to shiver.

"It's pretty quiet out here," from Broussard.

When I don't respond immediately, he says on a sigh, "Guess your not going to make it easy on me."

"Sir?"

"I'm trying to...pass the time. Make small talk. Get to know you a little, Ryan."

"Oh."

I look over at him. He's in full uniform, geared out like we are required to do for guard duty. Sexy stubble on his chin and eyes glittering at me through the semi-darkness. I'm not sure but I think his lips are tilted up in a half-smile.

"Are you planning to stay a while, sir?"

"I thought I'd keep you company tonight."

Butterflies explode in my stomach.

Keep calm, Ryan.

Broussard

Is there anything more alluring than Ryan decked out in full battle gear? I'm not sure. I told myself I was just going to come up and apologize then leave. But, now I am sitting beside her, wanting to prolong our contact. She's not making it easy though. Damn near the silent treatment. I can see the gears spinning in her head though.

Still waters run deep is the phrase I'd use to describe Ryan.

It's close to the end of our shift now, the sun just starting to peek over the horizon- the barest lightening of the sky.

Cars have been going along the main thoroughfare for half an hour now, and I watch and think about the people going about their daily lives as if their neighborhood is not an active warzone.

A gray sedan approaches the gate just to the right of us and about fifty yards out.

Ryan puts her rifle scope up to her eye while I listen in to the reports coming from the gate.

"Scheduled. Army officer Al Abir meeting with General Taal. Vehicle unknown. Proceed with caution, need visual and retina scan confirmation."

The air swells with vigilant apprehension.

The guard steps up to the car, the retina scan computer in his hands, while a bomb sniffing German shepherd and his handler do the standard checks around the vehicle.

A sudden rat-tat-tat of gunfire disrupts the routine. The guards take cover while the driver of the vehicle attempts to back up-but gets abruptly stopped by the pylons. The gunfire continues while I spot where it is coming from.

"One o'clock, Ryan."

She doesn't hesitate and opens fire at the insurgents standing behind the corner building.

A grenade comes from behind the wall and hits the car at the gate.

Officer Abir is probably toast, his car smoking, all the while gunfire chips away the concrete around the gatehouse.

The guards have successfully found cover in their fortifications, but we need to eliminate the threat so they can get back inside- a process at this FOB.

The communications are flying back and forth, and I am relaying information myself to the higher ups as Ryan keeps up a steady of stream of return fire.

She's suddenly standing up behind the firing wall, giving it all she's got.

I look into the street, where two insurgent's technicals have pulled to a stop, their guns pointed at our tower.

I see the operator of the left vehicle drop dead in my peripheral vision, just as I pull the trigger to hit the one on the right.

Somehow that fucker still manages to pull the trigger and the whoomp of a grenade launch reaches my ears.

Ryan pushes me down, inside the tower, her body weight following, as we fall uncontrolled in a jumbled evade maneuver. I see the back of her head hit the concrete floor as a dust cloud of mortar plumes out behind her.

I'm up and to her within seconds.

"Shit, Ryan, are you alright?"

The noise outside the wall has increased and judging by the radio comms flying back and forth the reinforcements have arrived.

Her eyes focus on me.

"Yea, I'm fine." She sits up and her eyes seem unfocused. I call for a medic.

"What about you," she says pointing to my neck.

I put my hand up to it and come away with a little trickle of blood.

"Yea, I'm fine," I tell her.

Abruptly all the gunfire stops, signaling the success of our backup. She starts laughing, while I just shake my head. Our medic and support have arrived.

She gets the once over, same as I do and a butterfly band aid is the extent of the medical attention I need. Ryan's eval seems to be taking a bit longer, so I listen in while the medic examines her. Checking for a possible concussion.

She refuses to go to the medical clinic for a scan.

"Go get cleaned up, Ryan." I tell her, "I'll handle the debriefing."

She nods just once, and slings her rifle over her shoulder.

I turn towards the medic.

"I'll keep an eye on her for concussion symptoms," I tell him.

He packs up his kit, and gives me a nod.

"You know where to report should she present any symptoms, Master Chief?"

"Sure do. Thanks kid."

26

Ryan

"Listen up, Pussies. We have a mission." Broussard breaks into our idle workout.

I set down the dumbbell in my hand and wipe the sweat off my face with the bottom of my shirt. T-Rex re-racks his weights with a clang, while the rest of the team follows suit to give their full undivided attention to the chief.

Per usual, my gut clenches at the sight of his handsome face. *Ignore it. Ignore it.* I repeat it over and over in my head, until T-Rex catches my eye. He gives me a questioning look since I still haven't moved from my spot in the corner of the tent. I roll my eyes and step into the impromptu huddle the guys created around Broussard.

"We are heading out tomorrow morning to the Death Pass. We'll be flushing out insurgents that have been making transports impossible." He continues, "We'll be inserting via chopper on the south side, while Seal Team Eight will insert on the north. Prepare for up to two weeks in rough terrain. Our trek should take us a week if we don't run into any issues. But we fully expect to engage the enemy at some point or points. Any questions?" He finishes.

His eyes connect with mine and the trill of attraction swirls in my stomach. After seconds tick by that feel like minutes he looks away breaking the connection. When nobody pipes in, he says, "Official briefing tonight twenty hundred."

"Hoo-Yah!" is the cheer that goes up at his last statement.

The huddle breaks up when Broussard gives a head nod and leaves out the tent.

T-Rex comes over to me.

"You ready to get dirty, little chicky?" He asks me while sitting down on the weight bench.

"Hells yea, T. You know it won't be the first time."

He laughs at that. "And what's up with you and the chief?"

I look around to make sure none of the other guys are listening in to our conversation. Then ask, "What do you mean?"

He gives me a look that means he doesn't believe in my playing dumb look.

"I could cut the tension with a knife." He says.

"That's just in your head. There's no tension." I tell him. I now have the worry that everybody in the world can read my attraction to Broussard on my face. I grab my empty water bottle and spin out of the tent. No need to keep this conversation going. I nearly crash into Broussard in my haste to get away. My chest a hairs-breadth away from hitting his shoulder, I do a inelegant shuffle to stop the impact.

"Sorry, Chief." I say after regaining my balance.

"No worries, Ryan."

I nod my head an keep on walking.

117

Broussard

I watch Ryan disappear through the maze of tents and temporary buildings. She seemed out of sorts, but I couldn't imagine why. She had performed exceptionally well on every DA we've been on- I can't imagine that this one would make her scared or nervous. I fold up the orders I had been reviewing, and turn back into the tent. Let my eyes adjust to the shade. The scent of sweat and heat and dust assaults my nose.

I find T-Rex sitting over on one of the weight benches. I make my way over to him.

"What's up with Ryan?" I ask him. No need to beat around the bush.

"What you mean Chief?"

I scratch my chin and the stubble that has turned into a near beard there.

"She seemed off. I don't know- you think it's finally getting to her?" I ask him hoping I don't sound like an overly concerned boyfriend. Fuck. I don't ever ask any of the other guys if the shit we see or the situations we are in ever fuck with their minds- and I know for a fact that sometimes it does.

"Nah, I don't think that's the problem, Chief."

My jaw tightens while I wait for him to elaborate.

"Shit's just tough for her sometimes. Fuck – it's tough for all of us, but she's got a target on her back the size of Texas." He says.

I turn from him and look out the rolled back door of the tent. The slightest breeze ruffles the ties holding the canvas back. I guess shit's just getting to Ryan.

"I have zero sympathy. She may have not known what exactly she was signing up for, but she knew. Deep down she knew this isn't a cake walk."

I leave T with that.

27

Ryan

We are on our third day of the mission. I'm climbing a goat trail behind Broussard, my pack weighing my shoulders down and making my steps heavier than normal. The sun is beating down ferociously, and I am eager for it to dip lower in the sky to grant the cool reprieve that is night. We are surrounded by brown rocky landscape interrupted only by scrub brush and short bushes. A brown valley is below us, and all I see ahead are brown mountains and outcroppings.

I pause and unscrew the cap from the water flask on my hip. I raise it to my lips and take a sip of the sweet cool water. A sudden whizz and plunk into the dirt between Broussard and I spikes my adrenaline hard.

"TAKE COVER!" I yell as fall to the ground. I bring my rifle up to my shoulder and shimmy up the incline on my back. About twenty feet up I reach the only cover on this side of the mountain, a large boulder. I throw myself behind it and meet Broussard there. He is relaying coordinates.

"Team four, just received fire at 145-006AG3, over." He clicks off his comm and says, "Glad you could make it, Ryan."

"I never miss a party, sir." He turns and peeks back over the rock. I give a looksee to my right. I see the tip of Hanzo's boot peeking out the bottom of a gully thirty or so feet down the trail. Meaty must be with him even though I can't see him.

"Sound off," Broussard orders into our shared comms.

The team all comes in with their statuses- all ok. Another pot shot hits the dirt between our rock and Meaty and Hanzo's location.

"They're just letting us know their here. For some reason they either can't see us or aim like shit."

I agree with Broussard. We are silent for a few moments. He sits back down beside me, no longer on high alert after a few minutes go by without another shot. I try not to notice that our shoulders and hips are rubbing against each other- the necessity of taking cover behind such a small boulder.

"You see where those shots come from, Ryan?"

"No Sir."

"Neither did I."

We are quiet a few minutes more waiting for another shot. Nothing happens.

"What do you think, Ryan?"

I was flattered that he was asking my opinion. "I think we either get a fix on their location or wait 'em out."

He peeks back over the rock. I get to my knees and do the same. Nothing to be seen on the opposite hill, just dirt, rocks and bushes. Wherever these fuckers are they are hiding good. Broussard sits back down behind the rock. I do the same.

"All right, ladies. Get comfortable. We are going to wait till dark to get a move on."

I settle in a bit more. The silence between Broussard and I is comfortable. About twenty minutes goes by before another errant shot is heard.

"Everybody good?" Broussard asks over the line.

A sequence of affirmatives echoes in my earpiece.

"Seems like we'll be here a while."

"Yea, Chief."

"You ever talk in complete paragraphs, Ryan?"

"Yes sir." My ironic statement slips out before I have a minute to sensor. I do usually talk a fair amount- around teammates I'm comfortable with. But around Chief Broussard my tongue and brain seem to get mixed up and I keep silent for fear of saying something I might regret later on. It's also my defense mechanism for denying the attraction I feel toward him.

We are both looking to the rock above us. An hour goes by. I have to shift my weight and move my position a bit because my butt cheek and foot were both asleep. It causes me to lean into Broussard a bit. I can feel the heat of his arm through the sleeve of my fatigues.

"Should be dark in about forty-five minutes." He says.

"Yes sir." is my response.

"Get your night vision goggles ready. We are going to wait about twenty minutes after dark to move."

"Yes sir."

"That's getting really fucking annoying, Ryan."

I stay quiet not wanting to piss him off any more.

"Seriously, what the fuck Ryan? Why aren't you home baking cookies for the PTA or some shit?"

I'm taken aback by his question. It came out of left field. I look into his eyes. They're green and sparking in the afternoon light. I look away into the rocky terrain before me. I see, not the rocks and dirt, but I see David's grave. I am not sharing that with Broussard.

"I'm not cut out for baking fucking cookies, Master Chief."

He huffs out a breath and says quietly, "Don't I know it."

That's the end of our conversation until another shot echoes of the rock walls. It's a bit closer. I take position behind the rock again. I scan the hill across from us. There- a shadow moving between two outcroppings.

"Master Chief. I have visual at ten o'clock, approximately fifty yards from the big boulder."

Broussard is beside me holding the binoculars up to his face.

"You got a shot?"

"Not yet."

We wait a few moments, and that fucker pops out from the hole he was in and starts a scuttle to a big rock- he's holding a RPG and has a rifle slung over his back.

I squeeze my trigger and he drops. Solid chest shot. I keep him in sight through the rifle scope. He's not moving.

"I think that's a confirmed kill, Ryan."

"Ten-four, Master Chief." I keep scanning the terrain.

I don't know if this was a lone wolf operator or he had friends. Thirty minutes goes by without further shots or tangos coming out. The sun is almost gone completely below the horizon, so I sit back down behind the boulder to get my night vision goggles from out of my pack.

"You ever think about sniper school, Ryan?"

I pull the wrapper from a granola bar and take a bite while contemplating his question.

"Honestly sir, it's just an honor to be on the Team. I never thought past making it here."

"Well maybe once this tour is over, I'll recommend you."

28

We our in our last month of deployment. Our team has been working systematically with the marines to clear sections of the city, blasting out pockets of insurgents. In the early morning hours, we muster up before heading out into our transports.

As I'm checking my ammo, loading a couple extra clips into my side pockets, Broussard's voice comes in through my headset.

"Ryan, Don't forget, your backing up B team on the clearing."

I look up to see him climbing into his Humvee, watching me across the expanse of dirt parking lot. Ever since the bomb incident as I call it, he always seems to go to extra effort to stress the orders to me- like he thinks I might disobey. A, "Ten-four, Master chief," is all I reply. I can follow orders just as well as the next guy. I climb in the transport nearest me.

We are split into four groups of four for clearing an industrial complex designated critical infrastructure (meaning we can't just blow it to pieces with any insurgents that may be inside it). Meaty is our point man, then Centennial, T-Rex and finally me.

The insert is flawless, and I run behind my team, gun at the ready. We reach the back half of the building that is our section to clear, and enter. It is a fairly small space, industrial, with metal walls, grate steps, and near darkness- only lit by the red emergency lighting spaced evenly down the corridor. So, somebody found out we were coming and activated the emergency lights. Good to know we won't be unexpected.

I follow T's back, doing sweeps left, right and behind us. We clear three offices and two store rooms, before going down to the next level, where some type of machinery is housed.

Once there, I file in behind my team, Meaty and Cent are already through the far door and into the next section of the machine room. Just as T's back disappears into the same space, a displacement of light or air alerts me to a presence behind me. Before I can spin and check it out, a sharp pain explodes in my right shoulder- driven in by the weight of a man now on my back. I spin quickly and bring my gun up between us, pulling the trigger while looking into the grimy face of a man with vicious intent in his eyes. He seems as startled as me when he pulls back and places his hand against his stomach and the wound there. He takes a step towards me and I put my rifle up to my shoulder and hit him with another shot in the chest. He goes down this time. The gunshots are muffled pops thanks the to silencer on the end of my rifle.

Death is ugly and raw and quick.

My team is back circling me, looking for any more threats. Meaty takes the tango's pulse and shakes his head. My shoulder is now screaming, the adrenaline wearing down but I hear Broussard's voice in my ear over the com, "Report Ryan. NOW."

"Sir, one tango down. I'm good." My voice sounds a little shaky even to me. Another pump of adrenaline floods my system and I start to shake. Shock maybe?

I look up from the ghastly blood pooling around the body and meet T-Rex's gaze. Only he's looking directly over my right shoulder, as he says, "Shit Ry." Then speaks into his com, "We need a medic."

I immediately cut in. "I don't need a fucking medic. Let's finish this."

Broussard is on the line, "What the fuck is going on down there? Give me a status."

I reach up with my left hand and touch the hilt of a knife protruding out of my shoulder. Fuck. It went in perfectly between the seam of my Kevlar vest at the top and back of my shoulder.

"It's good. I'm fine," I tell T-Rex and Meaty. I don't even turn my head to look at it, knowing if I do the panic might have me passing out. I got shaky legs, but I just need a minute to get more oxygen to my brain. I take deep breaths.

They both give me looks like I'm nuts.

Broussard breaks impatiently through the line, "I said give me a fucking status."

Meaty makes the decision. "Sir, we are in the southwest machine room. And now clear. Coming topside."

The other three teams chime in with their positions and status. Everything is just about wrapped up, the building clear and I fall in to go topside- this time T is behind me bringing up the rear.

Climbing the steps to get out the machine room, I'm seeing black stars dance in my vision and I start to feel the trickle of blood down my right side soaking my shirt. I experimentally try to lift my arm and only succeed in nearly passing out. I take a few more deep breaths. I'm still walking so that's a plus.

When we get to the top, activity is everywhere. A helo has landed in the dirt courtyard, it's blades whooping slowly. All the insurgents are restrained and sitting in a line awaiting pick up, while other team members are guarding them and organizing extraction. The element of surprise was on our side.

"T," I turn to him before we cross to where Broussard is standing, talking on the comm. "You got to pull it out. I won't be able to get the leverage."

"Just wait for Hanzo, girly."

"Fuck no. I can't wait for Hanzo. I need it out now. Don't you see? I'll be out if this is bad. I got to fix this…"

Broussard

As I send in the last confirmation to base of our successful mission, I see Ryan and T-Rex arguing about twenty five yards from me- Meaty and Cent standing by with their dicks in their hands. I'm fucking pissed about whatever went down with them and jog over there to give them new orders, and put a band aid on whatever boo-boo Ryan's got.

I'm about fifteen feet away when I see Ryan reach up and pull a bloody knife from her shoulder, then go down to her knees. It plays out in slow-mo from my point of view. T catches her and gently lays her on the deck. My stomach drops. I'm by her side and she's flat passed out, face as white as a ghost. "What the fuck, Lockwood?" I use T-Rex's real name as I start triage. "Hanzo!" I bark. And from somewhere he joins us, and we quickly get Ryan field dressed and on the helo.

As we chopper back to our FOB, I watch the medics set up an IV drip and cut away her Kevlar, her uniform. Taking her blood pressure, heart rate and relaying it back to their team on standby. I'm near sick to my stomach watching as her face, so usually full of fire and spirit, is still with grayness. Here's what I've been waiting for all along. A reason to have Ryan off the team. It doesn't feel satisfying or right. I just feel empty and like someone snatched away my prize.

Ryan

I'm shipped to a hospital in Germany for surgery and rehab. It takes three months to fix the torn tendons and ligaments in my shoulder and make it back stateside. Once there, it only takes a week for the honorable discharge to come through and my exit paperwork to be completed. It's signed by my commander, Master Chief Eric J. Broussard.

PART III

Soup Sandwich

29

Our hands bump as we reach for the same shot glass.

I move my hand one shot glass over and look up into Broussard's hazel eyes.

The waitress moves on with the tray full of shots down the bar. I hold the whiskey in my hands, studying the warm honey liquid, ignoring the solid warm man next to me, crowding my space.

T's wife takes the stage. Not literally, but she does step up on top of an industrial strength bucket with the help of one of the guys.

The quiet murmurings of the crowd quiet down, giving her the floor.

She balances with her right hand and holds her left aloft with a shot glass. Despite her red rimmed eyes that are shimmering in the low light of the bar, she clears her throat and begins with a clear voice.

"This is for T. Our brother, my husband, our protector. We love you."

She throws her shot back and we all follow suit.

The whiskey burns a warm path down my throat. Smooth, but probably because I had had two others before this one.

In the interlude, a quiet mournful song kicks on over the speakers, and some of the talk picks back up.

I place my empty shot glass on the bar, and the bartender picks up the empties with efficient dexterity, then adeptly begins lining up another round.

I watch the shellacked wood bar in front of me. But my mind's elsewhere, seeing T-Rex's face laughing in my memories.

Feet gripping the sand, the wetness, more compact, harder than any concrete, pounding, pounding my feet on it. I hear T's labored breathing behind me. See five of the team's backs up ahead of me... maybe slowly pulling away. I turn and start running backwards.

"C'mon T- you ugly mother fucker!"

My outburst most likely spurred by a runner's high- I would take advantage of it while it lasted.

I feel T behind me, closer, then drawing even. I kick my legs harder, unable to suck down enough oxygen for my renewed breath, but still keep pumping my legs, sucking air when I can. Soon we are passing Gonzalez.

Then Butters.

Maybe a mile and half left. A quarter of that up the sand dunes, to the real concrete, perhaps the hardest part.

There's two body-shaped figures in front of us now. The front two nowhere to be seen. I'm good being middle of the pack. I'm good middle of the pack. I repeat it in time to my foot falls. Soon T is falling behind me, but I keep up my pace. Before I know it, I'm back at the parking lot, Broussard, Evans and Meaty already there.

T comes in a minute and half behind me with Hanzo. I've got my breath now, and in my endorphin induced state I run up to him and start slapping his shoulders.

"You sexy mother fucker! You large piece of shit! Who's the man?!?! Who's the man?"

He grabs my upper arms, stopping my slaps. Throwing me over his shoulder and then swinging me down in some type of funny dance move.

"Damn. Kid!. Damn." He sets me on my feet, and I meet his high five, and then his low five.

"Ryan."

Broussard's voice brings me solidly back to now. The scarred wood bar before me, the funeral of a good man behind me.

"Yea?"

I looked up from my empty shot glass. Into his eyes. Anger has my hands curling around the glass.

"Can I talk to you a minute?"

"Yea."

I slide off the stool and follow him, the crowd now thinner, into the hallway leading back to the restrooms. He motions for me to proceed him down the hall.

I walk past him and stop just past the restrooms - it is private enough.

This man - with the achingly handsome face that gives my stomach butterflies- I hate him. With one swipe of his signature he utterly destroyed my life- erased all the hard work I had done, to nothing. And now, our friend, our teammate, our brother, suffered the worst fate. A shortened life.

I'm not saying my presence on the team could have changed the outcome. Hell, I could have died instead of T. I should have died instead of T. I have nothing, need nothing, am nothing.

But this man has robbed me of any chances. This man now short-pacing in front of me. One hand on his hip, the other sliding through his hair. The crispness of his uniform - reminding me of so much- but my failures most of all.

He stops in front of me. Arms crossed, legs braced. Head cocked to one side as he stares at my face.

I have to look away- although I hate him and the decisions he's made, I see a pain in his eyes. And I am not ready to forgive him.

"I'm Sorry, Ryan. God, I'm so sorry. I know how close you and T were."

I don't want to acknowledge his anguish. I cross my arms in front of my chest.

"Yea, aren't we all?"

It's a shit response, I know. But I really don't trust myself to say anything else. Ever since I stepped off that bar stool I've had the urge to point my feet out the door.

"Dammit Ry."

He grabs me by the back of my arms and brings our faces millimeters apart.

I can see all the varying shades of green and gold in his irises, swirling with hurt and maybe anger.

"Don't shut me out on this. I need to know."

He punctuates his words with a little shake.

"Did you have a thing for T? Did you love him?"

His words make me see red. I uncross my arms and push with all my might against his chest.

The surprise of my sudden move has him stepping back a few steps. I follow on my own offensive, pointing my finger in his chest.

"You fucking asshole! How can you fucking ask me that question? AT HIS FUCKING FUNERAL?"

It wasn't technically his funeral, but just the same.

He grabs the wrist of my pointing hand.

I stupidly yank it back towards me- instinct. Broussard takes advantage of my unbalance, aided by the shots I downed earlier and this insane pair of high heels, and grabs the wrist of my other hand, spinning me so my back is against the wall. His body solidly in front of me. The whiskey, my anger, his nearness -it's all swirling in my gut in a confusing and volatile mix. He pulls my right hand above my head and leans in close.

"Those types of reactions are an answer in and of themselves."

My heartbeat thunders in my chest. Adrenaline is flowing into my system. I don't like being cornered. And right now there is only one response. Fight.

"Fuck you."

I thrust my knee upwards, but he deftly deflects and pins my left hand above my head with my right. His lower body is now pinning my own to the wall.

I look down to where his erection is pressing into my stomach. Battle boner. I feel an answering reaction in my own lower body.

I buck against him and jerk my hands down to try and get him to release me.

No dice. My hands remain trapped above my head. I lift my eyes to his.

Our breaths mingle in the shared space between our lips. His eyes are blazing.

I think we both lean in at the same time - our lips crashing together and tongues swirling.

This kiss is not gentle. He starts to pull back, but I bite his lower lip.

He growls and pushes me back against the wall, thrusting his tongue back against my own, and as my head hits the wall, I hear my own grunt, the pain is what I need, so I don't pull away.

We are fighting for dominance in our kiss. Punishing each other for being alive when a good man is dead. Feeling when we should be numb.

Instinct has me lifting my right leg and wrapping it around his hip. My skirt rides up. I want his dick rubbing the ache between my legs, I want him impossibly closer.

A yellow light falls across my eyelids. It is as effective as the flash of a nuclear bomb going off. Both of us pull apart quickly.

The door to the bathroom shuts and whomever went in there is either oblivious to our make out session or politely ignoring us.

Broussard releases my wrists.

In the intimate darkness, my pain, my anger, and the all too alive lust has me answering Broussard's question as I step around him to leave.

"T was many things to me, a friend, a confidant, a brother...but I never..." I'm not sure how to go on.

He's still facing the wall, head down, one palm braced against it.

"I get it Ryan."

I nod my head once in the affirmative even though he can't see and keep on walking.

Back in the bar area there's only a dozen or so people left milling about. Jordan is putting her coat on with the help of about four people. No reason for me to stick around.

I open my clutch, pull out my cell and request a ride.

I will not think about what had just happened with Broussard. Even though my lips are currently tingling, my face hot, and my hands and legs shaky.

I step out of the pub to wait for the car on the curb. A little after midnight, and a few smokers are posted against the wall.

The pub is far enough from the main thoroughfares not to really have any street traffic this time of night.

I close my eyes and take a deep breath. God, Broussard smelled heavenly. Even now that I am nowhere near him - his clean scent lingers in my memory making me think about running my nose up the strong column of his neck, breathing his warmth in. My lips are buzzing in pain.

A car turns the corner, it's my ride.

Just as it pulls to a stop in front of the sidewalk real estate I had been occupying, a body brushes up against my back while a hand reaches past me for the door handle.

I spastically jump to the left.

"Jesus!" I exclaim at the same time I realize it's Broussard, "You scared the crap out of me."

He smirks and indicates the car.

"Share one with me?"

Without thought I give a, "Yea, ok." Damn whiskey. It knows I'm full of anger, nearly vibrating with it, and I could use a target. I climb in.

As Broussard follows me in, I tell the driver, "The Hyatt please."

I turn towards Broussard, expecting him to shoot off his destination.

He smiles at me.

"Me too."

I might have guessed. After all, my father had booked the room for me and of course the Navy guys all have one preferred hotel.

It is a ten-minute car ride. I can survive. No mentioning the kiss. People do crazy things when they're grieving. Right? Not that I am ready to forgive him- but that's probably what prompted Broussard's crazy line of questioning - grief. And also, that crazy kiss.

He seems content to ride in silence. I give a sigh in relief. Our last two encounters had not been my proudest moments. On the back of my eyelids I replay when I last saw him. The memory has my shoulder aching in pain. I reach up and give it a rub.

Obviously, when it comes to Chief Eric Broussard I have some unresolved resentment issues and some newly identified lust ones.

Our driver pulls up in front of the hotel lobby.

I pull a tip out of my clutch, but Broussard puts his hand on my wrist and pushes his ready cash through the partition.

I snap my clutch closed, and open the door on my left. No way am I sliding across the seat after him, even if it means I have to step out onto the street. This late at night there aren't any cars anyway.

The evening lights are blurred in the evening mists, the spring air chill. My fire seems to seep out just like that, my inner burn banked. Replaced by engulfing sadness.

I speed walk to the front door so Broussard can't pull the gentleman routine on me.

I'm through and at the elevator bank before he clears the door behind me. I press the button.

I am not in a rush. I just don't want to remain in the lingering awkwardness and I want to be alone, just in case I...well I can't even admit it to myself. I'm not going to cry. Stone heart and all that.

I press the up button again.

"You know, Ryan. It seems you are trying to escape me."

The elevator doors ding open.

I step in and press the button for floor three. I look back at Broussard- who follows me on the elevator and is now leaning back against the wall.

"Same floor as you, I have to see a lady to her door."

I scoff as the door closes.

"This is not a date, and you fucking know I am perfectly capable of taking care of myself, and you sure as fuck don't have to see me to my 'door'."

I finger quote when I say door. Just like that my anger is back.

He's not laughing. In fact he's loosening his tie and looking up at the numbers above the door with a tense face- jaw locked.

"I know Ryan. It's just ingrained in me."

I sigh. There's probably no dissuading him now.

The door opens to my floor. I step out and head down the carpeted hallway towards my room, pulling my key card out as I walk.

"Well, it's been swell, Chief."

I stick my key card in the slot on the door.

His hand comes down on my wrist again, stopping me from pulling the card back out.

I stare a minute at his square nails, and his square fingers, placed on my wrist, accentuating the more feminine line of mine.

This is my wrist. Caressed by his warm fingers. It even looks delicate beneath his fingers.

I lift my eyes to his over my shoulder. I can't read what's in them.

He curls his fingers all the way around my wrist and gives it a squeeze. He steps into my space and breathes down my neck with a warm breath. The mint and whiskey smell has me curling my toes.

This. This is chasing away my numbness. Reminding me I'm alive.

I turn around.

Before thinking, before analyzing, I tilt my head up and meet his lips with my own. I close my eyes and sink into the sensations. His tongue tangling with mine. His hand -hot- starting at my shoulder and trailing down my back, down, down to caress the curve above my ass, down to cup my cheek, and lift, so in repeat of earlier, my leg is persuaded to come up and hitch around his hip. My groin perfectly cups his erection. He rolls his hips and I moan in frustration. We are so close, yet so far away.

I slip my fingers in the collar of his jacket, the warmth of his neck delicious at my fingertips.

The door lock clicks behind me, and suddenly the pressure at my back is gone as the door swing opens.

I pull back from Broussard, and slowly disentangle my arms, my legs from his frame.

I press my tingling lips together and hum and sigh at the same time.

His face looks...lusty and focused, his breathing uneven. His right arm is up against the door jam, bent at the elbow so he leans into the doorway, his feet firmly planted on the outside of the room.

I take a deep breath and grab his jacket and pull him all the way towards me, across the threshold, into the security of the dark room and closer to my body.

One step, two, backwards while I unbutton his jacket with singular focus, not meeting his eyes, not really knowing where I am going with this.

His movements are hesitant, only following where I lead. His arms lax by his side.

I push his jacket off, and slip his tie all the way through his collar.

"Ryan…" he starts, as I push the first button on his shirt through the hole.

"Yes?" I question, starting on the next hole.

He clears his throat, "Nothing."

And with that word, he's all in.

He grabs my upper arms, and kicks the door closed. Eyes blazing into mine.

You better be sure, Ryan. You better be fuckin' sure."

A dose of reality hits me like cold ice water. I turn and pull away from him.

I was what? Going to use Broussard for one night of I'm alive sex? Sure, if I admit it to myself (which I never do) I have been attracted to this man since the moment our eyes collided the first day we met. I turn my back on him and sit on the edge of the bed, sliding my sling backs off, first one heel then the other - ignoring the looming male presence leaning against the wall and watching me.

I rub the arch of my foot and look up at Broussard. His jaw is clenched, his eyes locked on me and my gut clenches at being the single object of his gaze.

The longing pulls down to my loins and I know I want this man. He's no longer my commander, or anything to me. I can take advantage, get him out of my system, and move on. He's a man I want, and I can make this happen.

I stand up and walk into his space. Run my hand up his deliciously defined peck. Feel the warm steel of his muscles. Wrap my hand around the back of his neck and pull him down to meet my lips. The first press of our lips is tentative, but when I swipe my tongue along his lip, his restraint is broken. Our tongues are now mingling in a ferocious unleashing of passion.

I'm not holding back any longer- I spring to wrap both my legs around him. He anticipates my move and catches my butt - his warm palms supporting me.

Our tongues tangle, and before I know it, he places my butt on the little desk next to the TV and he's standing between my thighs - the slit in my skirt ripping as it rides higher on my thighs.

I growl at the inferiority of it. Placing my hands behind me I launch at him tumbling him backwards to the bed.

I quickly unbuckle his belt, but before I can reach the button on his fly he has me rolled to my back in a smooth maneuver as he nips at the column of my throat.

I am momentarily distracted by the pleasure/pain his kiss-nips engulf me in. I'm mindlessly grinding against his groin, while holding onto the strong column of his neck.

He lavishes attention on top of my breasts, now exposed. When had I lost my shirt?

He pulls my right breast out of it's silky cup and sucks the nipple gently. I hum with satisfaction. His warm palm against my flesh, it's beyond fantastic. I've got his pants completely unbuttoned now, and as I slide my hands just inside the waistband of his boxers, grabbing his dick a little enthusiastically, he gives the skin next to my nipple a bite in admonishment.

At my breast, he breathes, "Careful sweetheart, it's liable to explode if you pull the pin."

I give it another, gentler squeeze. A stroke.

It's warm steel in my hand, big. Bigger than David.

No. Don't think of David now. He's dead.

I pull my hands out of his pants, sliding them up the cut "V" ropes at his hips, his abs, and up to his chest where I push his shoulders in silent communication for him to roll to his back.

He does and I scoot down between his splayed legs, pulling his shoes off, then his socks. Trailing my hands up the inside of his thighs to the top of his pants. I tug at the waist and again he understands what I want.

He lifts his hips and in one backward glide his pants and boxers are gone.

A sigh escapes me at the beautiful man laid out before me in the low light. His muscles so well-defined. His dick, thick and jutting. I curl my hands into fists at my sides. I want to touch all of him. Run my tongue along all his muscles, and ride him till I die from orgasm. My pussy clenches and creams in anticipation.

His eyes meet mine. His are hooded, and maybe a bit weary.

I smirk at him. He's the vulnerable one now.

I straddle him as he sits up. It brings my silk panties in direct contact with him. Hot steel directly against my center. A low moan rolls from the bottom of my throat. His hands glide up the outside of my arms, to the top of my shoulders then he brings my bra straps down in the sweep of his hands. He pulls me closer - his arms steel bands holding me close to his hot embrace. He tilts his head up, offering a kiss. I have the power now. To take the kiss he is offering me. And to take everything else he is offering me. I don't immediately give him the kiss he is asking for, in his impatience, he growls and dips his head to bite at the base of my throat. My bra disappears. The heat and warmth of my breasts pressing against his chest...it's heaven. His hands glide around my rib cage, cupping my breasts.

I sway forward hoping he'll bring his mouth to them again. He doesn't disappoint.

My jaw, my neck, and my breasts all receive his attention. His hands are roaming my body, warming it, bringing it alive.

I reach for his dick again. Before I can get my hands lowered from his neck and chest- where I was doing my own roaming- he grabs my wrists and flips me back on the bed, pinning my wrists above my head. I feel a pinch in my right shoulder. But I ignore the pain.

He's breathing heavily, and pulls my bunched-up skirt from my hips with one hand. My panties are gone next. He then uses his hand to place his dick, just the head, within the folds of my pussy. It's wet enough that when he thrusts his hips in a tiny movement it glides up through my folds up, up, to hit my clit. He retreats and does it again.

The thickness of his dick spans the spread of my pussy. I'm watching it and him- the view enthralling and exhilarating. The pleasure and pressure building deep within my womb.

I pull my hands up against his hold, and curl my tail bone so that on his next thrust he's poised to enter me.

He abruptly lets go of my hands, and drops his head to my hip, sucking in air quickly.

I whimper at the loss of that magnificent phallus at my entrance.

"Shit, Ryan. Two seconds. I need a..."

I bring my hands awkwardly to loosely cover my chest.

Why did he stop? A disappointment I can't control is rolling through my head.

He pulls all the way away from me and stands at the end of the bed, scanning the floor. He grabs his pants in triumph, and pulls his wallet from the back pocket.

He uses his teeth to rip the packet open and without pause, rolls the condom down his substantial length.

He looks up, meets my eyes and gives me a lopsided grin.

I'm dumbstruck by how the smile transforms his face.

Leaning down, he places one palm at my hip on the mattress, then climbs up my body, coming to a stop once we are chest to chest, groin to groin.

His right hand cups my left breast, his thumb brushing the the tattoo underneath it.

He breathes at my lips, 'Semper fi?"

The reminder is all too real. I suck in a breath. I grab his hand cupping my breast and hold it there, while bumping his pelvis with my own. Bringing my lips, my tongue to meet his own, I want this to forget. To forget David. Forget T. Forget the pain.

His dick is poised at my entrance, and I take that last bit of control and thrust my hips at an angle, taking another half inch into my entrance.
He takes the hint and thrusts all the way home.

I groan. I can't hold back. The ecstasy of being filled-almost painful. It steals my breath away.

"Shit, Ryan. You're so tight."

I squeeze my eyes shut at his words. Tilt my hips in a short rocking movement.

Again he understands my cues, and rocks against me hitting my clit -oh so good. Five rocks, ten, I lose count.

He grabs my chin.

"Open your eyes, Ryan."

I do. He's rocking, rocking, rocking against my clit.

"Tell me who's fucking you so good."

I do, "You are, god you arrrrghhhh."

He growls and pinches my nipple.

I come. My muscles clenching him in ecstasy. I don't want to ever let go of how full I am, how alive I am. All muscles clenched, pleasure spiraling down and then out. Ten seconds, fifteen, twenty. I don't care. I just had a phenomenal orgasm and I don't want it to go.

I give an experimental tilt of my hips. Yep, dick still in pussy. An aftershock of pleasure echoes within my womb.

He pulls out and I'm flipped onto my stomach. I reach behind me, I need skin contact. My fingers graze his muscular thighs; he tilts my hips up, and thrusts. I'm immediately penetrated, the surprise, the pleasure spinning me to new heights. A sudden slap- stinging heat warming my right ass cheek.

I pull away, but not enough to completely disengage him. He grabs both my wrists and pulls me back to meet his thrusts.

Another orgasm has me screaming into the pillow. I'm aware of Broussard, on a peripheral level, he thrusts only twice after I come, and has his own orgasm. I am just a pile of gelatinous goo, muscles, inside and out, quivering in pleasure.

He pulls out, and lands beside me, on his back, one arm thrown over his head, the other gripping the condom to his dick.

I let my legs relax, sliding down to my stomach and turning my head from Broussard's panting form next to me. What have I done?

He gets up, and I hear the light click on, the faucet start and stop, then the shower.

Good. Maybe if I lay here, he'll get cleaned up and kiss me goodbye, and be gone. No more embarrassment, no more Broussard. A tinge of sadness flows through me at this thought. No. I will not bring it to the front of my thoughts, I will not give it attention, and thus substance.

A warm hand wraps around my ankle pulling me backwards along the bed.

"C'mon Ryan. Shower time."

"Ughhh…" I groan unhappily back at him.

He drops my leg when my bottom half is on the floor.

I look back and just glimpse his apple-bottom and broad shoulders going through the door into the bathroom.

"Don't make me come get you," he hollers from the bathroom.

I push up from the bed - there's a soreness and slickness between my thighs. A shower sounds heavenly.

30

I put my hand underneath the water - it's hot and ready- just missing my girl.

Shit! I can't think of her that way. Just yet. Right? After she was discharged, we haven't been in contact at all. I was kept appraised of her status, the surgery and rehab on her shoulder, but other than that, I never reached out.

I turn, readying to go get her and drop her in the shower if need be, but she's there, standing silently in the doorway, looking for all the world just so sexily fucked-messy hair, red, swollen lips. Her body language is hesitant though, she's got one arm crossed in front of her chest, the other dangling down by her side. She's looking down at the floor.

I hold my hand out to her, she takes it, and I guide her into the shower enclosure, adjusting the spray so it doesn't hit her squarely in the face.

I look down at her face. She's staring solidly at my chest.

I've never known Ryan to be so...timid. After sex people get awkward. But...Ryan. Well, this is surprising the shit out of me.

I grab the bar of soap from the cubby, and spin her around and start washing her back.

Her shoulders are slender and feminine. With the exception of the four inch pink scar on her right shoulder - it's flawless. I continue washing, my gaze following my hands. Down her spine, to the most perfect ass I've ever seen- and it's currently sporting a bright red hand print. It's fucking beautiful seeing my mark on her. My dick jumps in happy response.

I trail the soap, my hand down into the middle of those two luscious globes, while kicking her feet apart, unbalancing her so that she throws her hands up against the tile in front of her to steady herself.

Her breathing is loud. I replace my hand with my now throbbing dick. It's sliding oh so good with the soapy lubricant in between the globes of her ass.

Fucccck. I'm going to come again.

Not wanting to leave Ryan behind, I reach around, grab her breast and give her nipple a tug.

She moans. I do it one more time, before dipping lower to her pussy.

The soap, the water and her moisture - combine in a pleasurable friction-reduced glide. I tease her outer lips, inner lips, never hitting her clit, all the while my dick is cradled by the softness of her backside.

She's writhing in my hand.

"Please, Eric...please…"

Damn. I think this is the first time she's called me by my first name. Hearing her use my name in tandem with a beg, It ratchets my own building pleasure up just a notch below orgasm.

Bringing my lips to the junction of her neck and shoulder, I look down the front of her- her soaped-up breasts, my hand between her thighs- it's a glorious sight.

"What do you want, Ryan? Tell me."

She doesn't pause in her writhing, in fact she leans her head back more solidly against my shoulder. Her eyes are squeezed shut, her face in concentration.

"Please...my clit..."

My balls draw up at her words, and I don't hesitate to give her what she's asking for. The instant my finger draws on that tight little bundle of nerves, she's pulsating in my arms. It's damn near the first simultaneous orgasm I've ever had- my cum splashing onto her lower back.

I take a second to catch my breath. I've curved my upper body around hers, my forearm braced against the wall supporting our slight lean into the wall.

I push away and reverse our positions so the stream of water is now coming from over my shoulder and hitting her back. I reach down to the bottom of the stall and pick up the soap, washing the mess I made away.

This woman I vowed to never touch. Too young, too sexy, too much attitude, and under my command. I hated the thought of her at first. But a begrudging admiration morphed into a simple pride, all throughout our deployment, she continually surprised me with her tenacity and abilities. But the probability of more situations where she might be hurt, my gut always clenches at the thought. The scar on her shoulder, I trace my fingers down it. More had happened. And well-maybe I'm not happy that it meant the end of her experiment- I am satisfied that she's safe stateside.

She spins in my arms, grabbing the soap out of my hand. Starts gliding those smooth warm hands up my pectorals, around my lats, down along my sides.

Wash. Rinse. Repeat- it's heaven.

I'm nearly catatonic after two orgasms. And I know, I know my time with her is limited. I've got just a half day, then I'm shipping back. I try to keep my eyes open, but the heat of the shower, combined with the stress of the day...I'm nearly sleeping on my feet.

The shower is switched off, and Ryan's there in a towel, holding my own out to me.

"Ryan. Let's go to bed. I'm beat."

I scrub the towel over my face, meet her gray eyes.
"Yes. Bed." she agrees.

31

Ryan

I lie in his arms, completely awake, and now completely sober.

Tomorrow I'm back to California, to a life that isn't a life. He's still got four or five months on his deployment. I'm not really sure... I've convinced myself that it's best if I distance myself from the details of my ex-team.

I take a deep breath. It's like laying here- I'm finally alive and I can't go back to sleep. Seven plus months I've been...absent. I recognize it as the depression it's been.

Now, at the touch of this man, he awakens me. I'm alive. His touch brought me back to life. And T - he's dead. My best friend, a man way more deserving than me, lies cold in the ground. I want to go back to numbness. I don't want this pain. I've felt it before, and it spurred me down a road that led to failure.

Damn Broussard.

I lift his arm from my shoulders and scoot across the bed- our legs no longer touching. I sit up and look back at his form. He's splayed out, stomach down, on arm cupping the pillow to his head, the other down by his side, one leg splayed out. I was, a moment ago, under that leg, under that arm.

His face, astonishingly younger in repose. He's not tensing his jaw or furrowing his brow. It's almost as if he is...smiling to himself.

I turn from him and run my hands through my hair, still slightly damp from the shower.
The clock is shining its red neon face brightly, 3:42AM.

I have a flight at seven AM. I run through the calculations in my head. One hour to get there. Six AM. One hour to get ready, five AM.

I'm close enough. Plus, I won't have to do all that mushy/awkward goodbye stuff with Broussard if I leave now.

I stand up, pull my bag into the bathroom with me. I'm not sneaking out.

I quietly brush my teeth and get dressed.

I go back to the room, allowing the light from the bathroom to illuminate what I need. Picking up my skirt, my shirt, my shoes, my cell phone charger, I place them all in my go bag.

I pull my cross trainers on, and leave my key card on the sideboard.

Take one last look at the sleeping male form on the bed. Broussard's got the blanket tucked up under his arms, and underneath it his chest rises and falls in deep rhythmic breaths. He has one masculine foot sticking out the bottom of the covers. Seeing him like this - vulnerable, relaxed- well it's a softer side of him I never would have thought existed. Like catching a glimpse of a unicorn under a rainbow.

Should I leave a note?

I've never been in this situation before. Mixed emotions of remorse, shame, and embarrassment crash through me.

I grab my bag and as quietly as I can exit through the door.

Broussard

I know a second before I open my eyes I'm the only one in the room. I groggily roll to my side and push up, swing my feet over the edge of the bed. I let my head fall into my hands for a moment and take a deep breath. "Fuck."

I say the one word out loud. It doesn't make me feel any better. I scrub my hands down my face and stand doing a slow scan of the room.

Yep. Her bag and cell phone charger are gone. I walk to the bathroom and look at the vanity - no toothbrush either. I turn on the faucet and splash some water on my face.

Look up into the mirror.

"Face it Broussie, there's a first time for everything." I turn off the faucet.

This just happens to be the first time a woman has left me without a goodbye after a night of great sex. The first time a woman has left me period.

I walk back in the room and start gathering my gear. I sit on the bed to pull on my pants. Put one leg through and pause as a thought crosses my mind.

Damn. I didn't want it to end this way.

I chuckle to myself. Really, should I have expected anything but the unexpected from Ryan?

Time for the burn portion of this turn and burn.

Pulling my cell out of my pocket, I see I've got two texts from Peanut.

Where u at Chief?

I had to leave rather hurriedly to catch Ryan as she was leaving the bar last night and didn't have a chance to signal that I was leaving to anyone.

1600.

The last was a simple reminder of our flight out time.

I pull on my shirt and take a look at the clock. It's not even nine AM - I have plenty of time to get back to my room, get changed and get something to eat before we roll out.

I take one last look around the room before I leave, just in case I missed a note or something. But it seems the only thing she left behind is her key card on the sideboard.

It's for the best, I tell myself, no awkward goodbyes or empty promises.

PART IV

FIDO

32

I've been looking at the same topography maps for about two hours, trying to find an insertion point that isn't stupidly vulnerable when Butters walks into the office.

I lean back in my chair happy for a break.

"Yo. Chief, you ain't gonna believe this shit."

He's got a face splitting grin on as he slaps a magazine down on the desk in front of me. It's not any magazine though-there's a pair of glorious naked tits split by the barrel of M4, staring up at me from the glossy page; but it's what's directly under one of those breasts that catches my eye - a semper fi tattoo. I think my heart stops beating.

No fucking way. I scan up to the face above the tits. Holy shit, it is Ryan.

Gloriously laid out on an American flag, naked as a jaybird, cradling the M4 with one hand just below her breast, the stock resting just at her waxed pussy. Her eyes in hooded desire, her other hand thrown up over her head. A look I would have thought not possible for her to make - had I not seen it myself the last night we were together. Her hair is blonde- so different from her own chestnut locks- but it's definitely sexy with a Cameron Diaz vibe. My dick rises to half-mast.

"Jesus fucking Christ. What the FUCK is this?"

I open the magazine all the way up from where Butters had it folded in half. It's Playboy. I flip past the centerfold, to the picture of Ryan three-fourths of the way in. The opposite page has an article titled, "Kicking ass and taking names in the Military- interview with one of the first woman to participate in active combat missions."

I flip the page without reading, my curiosity and dread mingling to see more pictures. I'm delighted to find there are...one black and white art photo, taken from behind, her face in profile. She's wearing a giant angel wing, just like the models on the Victoria's secret fashion show, but it's a bit more droopy and with black tinted feathers instead of all white. The scar on her right shoulder is standing out in huge relief- they must have added makeup to make it look like that. A fallen angel...how ironic.

Her perfect ass tapers into long glorious legs, perfectly formed and on display in a pair of fuck me heels. The background is some empty industrial warehouse. Damn. The imaging is as haunting, dramatic, and striking as much as it is beautiful.

The next image is another black and white, this time she's facing forward, her dog tags dangling between her bare breasts, the one wing just visible over her shoulder, her hands hooked into the panties at her hips- pulled provocatively low. Dark rimmed eyes, making love to the camera. Sharing this last page is four photos on the right margin, stacked one on top of another. The first, she's laying on her stomach on the flag again, her arms cushioning her head as we get to see down the back line of her body.

The second, she is standing up legs spread wide, shot from behind the flag draped over one shoulder, and her other arm in a T to her side holding the M4 by the barrel as the stock sits on the floor. The third she's laying on her back, biting down one a dog tag with a half smirk. And the final picture she's sitting on a rough wood pallet type box, dog tag and chain dangling from one wrist, wrapped like a damn rosary, palms together in prayer, elbows on knees and knees together feet wide. Her head down. It's poignant.

I flip one more time, but that's it. I flip back to the article and start reading. The first paragraph is the author's observations of meeting Ryan in person:

Meeting and photographing the magnanimous E. Ryan was one of the more challenging -and rewarding- assignments of my career. She's humble to the point of closed off. She's a risk taker, but hardly a thrill seeker. A spine of steel, a heart of gold, bad attitude and a quirky sense of almost-nerdy humor. Can women serve in the military? Ryan's proof they can.

Could the man have his nose any further up her ass? I keep reading. Standard first interview question, Why did you join the military?

I keep reading, and her response nearly floors me.

It's probably against woman code to say this, but I joined up because of a man. Not any man, Kurt, but my fiancé, David. I was in the middle of my second year of college, when he was killed in action. IED. After his funeral, I couldn't stand the thought of going back to "normal" life. So I joined up.

She had a fiancé? One she loved so much, she quit college to start a career in combat?

The next few questions and answers give the basic outline of her career path in the marines, leading to the question of why she joined the Navy and didn't just re-enlist with the Marines.

I had an opportunity, to do something women have been ostracized from since the creation of it; I was invited- on an experimental basis with six other women - to go through BUD/s. For civilians out there, this is the elite training program for SEALs. And did you make it through? I'm restricted by security protocols from answering that question.

The next several lines are more questions pertaining to where she's been the last two and half years since she left the marines. She doesn't give him any answers, but the line of questioning alludes to the fact that she graduated and was placed on a spec ops team.

The interview turns to a question about men and woman fraternizing in the military - has she ever...?

You know, there are so many brave, courageous and handsome men in the military-but I think of them all as my brothers-in-arms, that's it. There's been one exception, but I can't talk about it.

Damn. My heart stops and starts back up again. Am I the exception?

I read the rest of the article- the interviewer asking about the scar on her shoulder, how she managed to keep up with some of the most physically fit men on the planet, and how she feels about taking a stand, blazing a path as a woman in the male dominated military.

She answers each with depth, vulnerability and smidge of aloofness. The article closes with the writer thanking all military and their families for the heroic sacrifices they have made for freedom and country.

I flip the page and look at the pictures one more time.

Closing my eyes I see her that last night, below me, face concentrated in pleasure.

I sit back all the way in my chair and look up at Butters.

"Who else has seen this?"

"Just about everyone in C company. You know we get about thirty copies delivered each month in the care packages."

"Fuuuuuccck."

A feeling of protectiveness washes through me, and my stomach seems to drop at the news. A quick wash of anger comes next and I hold on to it. How could she be so fucking stupid?

I close the magazine with one hand. I can't acknowledge that this means anything. She hasn't broken any rules per se, and I'm sure the Naval higher-ups won't

be too happy with her, and her father being one of those-
He's probably doubly unhappy.

But for us, SEAL Team Four, this is just another day,
another hot ass naked chick holding a gun in the *Playboy*.

33

Ryan

I watch all the scantily clad women, gaily sipping champagne and cocktails in their "pajamas." I am beyond glad I ignored the dress code and went with what I felt might be right for one's own 'coming out' party - this month's playboy release party- thigh high soft leather boots with a wedge heel, black short-shorts (very feminine and edgy for me), and a plain dark gray t-shirt under a lightweight leather motorcycle jacket.

I'm sipping a glass of pinot grigio, a little terrible at first, but after the third sip I'm enjoying its refreshing acidity.

I'd already done my required hellos, and am just waiting for Kurt to show so I can say hello and head back to the hotel.

An athletic looking man steps in front of me.

"Excuse me, E. Ryan?"

"Yes?"

I meet his eyes -aquamarine blue. It's more startling for the fact that his skin is the color of a caramel latte.

"Alex Devereaux. I couldn't help but notice you standing over here all by yourself."

'Ha. Terrible come-on Alex. I've been surrounded all night long, this is the first breather I've had."

"Ahh. Well guess I don't have to try any more."

Despite myself, I feel my lips turn up in a return smile. I like his athletic build, his ready smile, his exotic look.

He sips his drink, while we look out at the crowd in companionable silence. Really, I should try to be more social. Make some chit-chat.

"So, what you thinkin' about?" It might be the wine turning me into a veritable chatty Cathy, but I feel the need to fill the silence with something. It's a social awkwardness I haven't felt in some time. Like I'm finally aware that I'm a woman in a social situation.

"All these girls, they need a good breakfast. You know what I mean?" He turns to me.

I give him a skeptical look.

"Waffles with chocolate chips, smothered in butter and syrup, sausage and hash browns, eggs over easy, toast with jam…"

He trails off and meets my eyes,

I bust out laughing at the same time he does.

"Damn! I'm just hungry! It's been a long day," he finishes up.

The words tumble from my mouth without thought, "Waffles sound awesome."

Sneaking away from a playboy mansion party is probably the opposite of what most people wish to do, but we do and find an authentic 24-hour diner. Gorging ourselves on waffles with chocolate shakes, coffee and hash browns, sausage and eggs over easy.

We discuss just about everything under the sun in the hour and half we consume our epic breakfast. Alex seems genuine. He admits to playing in the NFL, with the season set to start in a few weeks, he is just doing some different things, trainings and workouts while taking advantage of where career and money opportunities are taking him- namely Playboy mansion parties. He had grown up just this side of poor in New Orleans.

He's humble and flirty, in a half serious way.

"You see, visiting the playboy mansion, that's bucket list stuff I can tell my grandkids about one day."

I laugh at his term- bucket list.

"Yep, that's exactly what I'm going to tell my kids, posing in Playboy was a bucket list item."

He laughs, a good round solid laugh.

"Ryan! You know what? I like you!"

I tip my coffee cup to him and tell him, "I like you too, Devereaux."

He hasn't mentioned the pictures in Playboy once. Whether he's being tactful or has a canny ability to read my modesty, I'm not sure.

"Well, if I keep eating like this, I'm sure I'll look nothing like my photos."

"Shoot, if you keep eating like this, I might have to marry you!"

We both start laughing at that.

We languidly exit the diner, and Devereaux kindly drives me back to the hotel. We are both quiet on the ride, stuffed to the gills and just enjoying the silence.

At the door, he puts the car in park and pulls out his phone.

"Ryan, I've had a good time tonight- let me get your number so we can stay in touch. Maybe have another epic breakfast some day."

"Hey- anytime you want to treat me to an epic breakfast- I'm down."

We exchange numbers, and after a quick peck on the cheek, I exit the vehicle and head through the hotel doors. I turn around after going through the door, and see Alex is still sitting at the curb watching me.

I wave to him and he waves back, then puts the car in gear and pulls out into the street.

Gentleman to the core. Would Broussard see to it that I made it home ok? Of course.

161

Why am I even thinking about him? I'm annoyed with my inability to forget about him after several months. As I ride the hotel elevator up to my floor, I think back to that night and involuntarily shiver.

Give it up girl. It's not meant to be.

34

Maybe I should flip over. Or go for a dive in the pool. The sweat is trickling down my chest, the sun beating down in relentless heat on my face. But, I'm in that hazy moment between actually sleeping and fully aware. A shadow crosses over my face.

I pull back my hat and open my eyes. It's my sister, Kinsey toting an over the shoulder bag and holding the hand of her oldest, five-year-old Liberty.

"Everly. I need you to watch Liberty for a couple hours. Sean's mother is coming to visit and I need some time to clean the house."

Liberty smiles at me and in an angelic voice asks, "Can I go swimming, Auntie Everly?"

My sister picks up without missing a beat: "Her suit is in here." She slides the tote bag off her shoulder and continues, "Along with some sunscreen, snacks, floaties, juice...You can call me on my cell if you have any issues. But I'll have Sean pick her up on his way home from the office."

She lets go of her daughter's hand and bends down to be face to face with the kid.

I stand up. My brain finally kicks into gear.

"....listen to you're aunt. No running. No jumping. Wear your floaties. Put on sunscreen..." I interrupt her parental tirade to Liberty.

"I'm not a babysitter or a lifeguard. You can't just dump..." She spastically covers Liberty's ears and glares at me, but I continue, "...her on me and expect me not to have plans."

She stands up tall and comes in close.

"Do you have plans, Everly?" She asks in a nice controlled voice. Yea, plans to make a margarita right after my nap.

"I didn't think so." She says after my answering silence.

"Listen to me Everly. I need a break. A glass of wine while I sweep and vacuum and clean the toilets. Sean's mom is coming in tonight and I am STRESSED."

She emphasizes this by pointing her finger at me.

"You will do me this favor, because you love me, you love Liberty and so help me GAWD...because you have been a veritable slug since you got home a month ago!"

She huffs the last bit. Well. After the Playboy party, I just can't generate any energy to do, well anything. The CIA has been non-existent after their repeated attempts of persuasion, and my bank account has enough money in it for me to retire five times over- thanks to my portion of my mom's trust, my military paychecks that I literally never spent, and the deal with Playboy.

I take stock of my sister's pale face, dark circles under eyes surrounded by crazy mom hair- and it looks like she is wearing a scrunchie. Okay. Stressed woman. I look down at Liberty whose eyes are lit up with hope at the promise of an afternoon swimming- freaking angel face.

It's just a couple hours I tell myself. I can handle a five year old for a couple of hours. Shit, it can't be any worse than BUD/S, right? And I made it through that.

"Fine." I agree.

She bends back down to continue the parental deluge to Liberty, "...No peeing in the pool..."

I tune it out and retrieve the dropped tote bag in defeat.

It's three hours later when I have Liberty dried and napping on the couch that I dial Kinsey. Where is Sean? Her phone goes straight to voicemail so I type out an angry text message. *Sean hasn't shown up. Come pick up your kid.*

I play two levels on candy crush and still no response.

My irritation level climbs up several notches.

How can she just forget about Liberty? I take a deep breath and look around the guest house where I've been staying since I got back stateside. It's just one big open area with a king size bed- currently unmade- kitchen and bar with a little seating area that faces out to the pool. Liberty seems to be out cold on the couch there.

Maybe it wouldn't hurt to let her sleep a bit- probably by the time she wakes up I'll have heard from Kinsey or Sean will be here to pick her up.

My eyes fall back to the kitchen. It's a mess. Cups and takeout boxes line the counter tops. I guess I have been a bit of a recluse lately. I grab a trash bag from under the sink and began throwing away the empty pizza boxes and putting dishes in the sink.

Soon I'm pulled out of my cleaning frenzy by Liberty saying my name.

"Aunt Everly. I have to pee."

"Right. Bathroom is this way." Thank god she is potty trained. I didn't think to ask and I don't think any of my other nieces or nephew's are. I check my phone- no messages, and forty five minutes has gone by since I texted Kinsey.

Liberty distracts me from finishing another text message.

"Aunt Everly, I'm hungry."

Shit- It's getting to be dinner time and all I got in the refrigerator are some limes and tequila.

The good thing is – Kinsey and Sean's house is just two miles down the road.

Liberty and I can walk that no problem. Yea, I hadn't even bought a car since I've been back. I am Ms. irresponsibility. No rent. No car. No Problems, right?

"All right, Liberty- get your shoes on - we're going home."

"Can we get ice cream on the way?"

I have no idea where we would get ice cream on the walk- so I reply with, "Not before dinner."

She pulls a pouty face, but slips on her shoes.

A two mile walk later - during which I piggy-backed Liberty one and a half of- we arrive at Kinsey's. There is an unfamiliar vehicle in the driveway - must be the mother-in-law and thus the reason Kinsey didn't answer phone calls or text.

I knock but push my way into the entryway at the same time.

"Hello? Kinsey?"

The heavenly smells of a home-cooked Italian meal let me know there is someone in residence.

I set Liberty down. And she shoots off like a rocket towards the kitchen.

Since I now hear voices within, I follow at a more respectable adult pace.

The kitchen is gleaming clean and my sister picks up Liberty - who has rushed into her arms- in a fluid movement.

"Ahhh. Thank you Ryan. Sean is stuck in traffic....I was just about to text you."

A regal looking woman with blonde hair sprinkled with gray is sitting at the breakfast table. A glass of white wine in hand as she calls over to us, "And this is your mystery sister, Kinsey? The one I've yet to meet! Well come over here for an introduction, little lady!"

I don't think I've been called 'little' or 'lady' my whole life.

I walk over and shake her hand- she indicates a seat at the table.

"Sit down Everly. Have a glass of wine with us while we wait on Sean." I cringe inwardly again. No one in my family calls me Everly.

I reluctantly pull out a chair, while Kinsey places an empty glass in front of me and Mother-in-law pours from a chilled bottle sitting on the table. I guess wine is just as good as a margarita.

What passes in the next hour is a torture like none other, attempting to make small talk with a monster-in-law that is not even my own.

She's not even subtle about trying to set me up with Sean's younger brother, a twenty something finishing up his last year of law school. After I finish my glass of wine, I stand up to leave- even though Kinsey is giving me pleading looks to stay.

"Thanks for the wine. I'll see ya later."

Kinsey walks me to the door, "You sure you don't want to stay for dinner?"

I whisper back to her, "Gawd no. That woman makes the CIA look like amateurs. She's relentless."

Kinsey chuckles and pulls me in for a hug. "All right, Ryan. Thanks for today. I know I didn't approach it right, asking for your help, but it truly was a lifesaver."

She smiles a tired, but utterly grateful smile at me that is reminiscent of our mother.

I nod and walk down her front steps without a backward glance.

35

On the walk home my mind wanders. I should want
eat dinner with Kinsey and her beautiful family and eat
French bread drenched in homemade pasta sauce. I should
date Sean's brother the lawyer, right? I should be out
mingling with people, living life and...what? Somehow it all
just feels...not me. PTSD? I don't think so. But, if I'm
honest with myself I skip all the post exit therapist sessions
that are assigned. Even though I know I am making the
wrong steps, I just can't seem to muster up the energy to
face anything. I don't really like being told what to do, and
there's no structure or consequences for doing the right
things.

Once back to the pool/guest house I take out the ice
cream pint in the back of my freezer and stare miserably
down at the scoop and half that is left.

I pour a shot of vodka over it. And take a bite. It is
terrible. I root through the liquor cabinet and find some
Kahlua. Add a shot of that over my 'dessert.' My second
tasting is much better.

I plop down on the couch and flip through Facebook
on my phone. See, I tell myself, I can be social. I like a
photo of fluffy kittens in a slow-mo video being blown dry.
Scroll a bit more.

A pop-up informs me it's Butter's birthday. I click over to his page to give him some shit for being an old man.

There at the top of the page is: "Eric J. Broussard>Michael Knox."
And a gif of Paula Deen doing pushups. It is funny. I hover over the clickable blue name, "Eric J. Broussard."

Should I? We'd always kept everything professional and I am only friends online with a few of the team. But it is no longer my world. I feel a sadness wash over me like never before. I am not going back. I have spent the last month laying by the pool, sleeping when I wanted, eating what I wanted, drinking what I wanted - all in denial that I am out. I take a deep breath and click off the Facebook app. Shut down my phone.

What to do now? I guess I could...get a job. I tried to think back to what I wanted to do when I was in college. I searched back before I met David - I was a senior in high school then. What did I do besides ballet? I came up empty handed.

I take my empty bowl to the sink and attempt a plié. My knees crack and grate. My left has a pronounced pain at the front of the kneecap. Bad form. The rigors of running around in combat boots instead of ballet shoes probably does not put me into any kind of contention for a dance company.

I go to bed contemplating what I might be able to fill my time with.

36

The next day I hit the pavement for my first run since...well I can't be sure. It's just five and half grueling miles, but in that short time I realize I just got to start doing...something. It doesn't matter too much what it is, but just because I no longer have something to fight doesn't mean I have to wither away. Of course, it may just be the endorphins talking, but I feel hopeful for the first time in a long time.

In the shower I wash the run sweat from my body. Pondering my next steps, but there seems to be no answers in the shower stall. I think back to how Broussard washed me that night in the hotel- reverently. I switch off the showerhead and grab a towel, disgusted with myself for how much I think of him sometimes. It's like I crave his stupid face looking at me with disapproval.

My phone beeps from wherever I left it.

I wrap the towel around my body and hunt for it.

I finally find it stuck between two couch cushions.

I know it's a long shot- but want to come up to Seattle for some breakfast? Is the message on the screen.

From Alex Devereaux.

I can't help but feel it's a sign. That I need to get on with my life. My civilian life. My romantic life.

Depends on what kind of breakfast you had in mind, I type back at him.

A moment passes where I am staring at the screen.

A Fall breakfast: pumpkin spice latte, pumpkin spice muffins, pumpkin spice waffles...you get the theme.

I type back a single reply, When? My brain registers that it is now September. Seems I have blurred over most of August, and maybe July and June too. The playboy party had been in May. Shit. I need to get it together.

I quickly Google the weather in Seattle- lows in the fifties. It'd be a welcome change from sunny southern California.

Broussard

A month has passed since Ryan showed up on my desk in all her naked playboy glory. I am like a crazy fiend, keeping the playboy shoved into the bottom of my footlocker, ignoring the temptation to look at it, whack off to it - a kind of self-inflicted torture.

It's Tuesday at twenty two hundred, the appointed hour I get to Skype with Luke. Dang kid is in 1st grade now, and I can hardly believe it's been six years since he came into the world.

I plug in the laptop to make sure I'll have enough power through the call and log in.

His face flashes on the screen after the first ring.

"HEY DAD! I got to touch a DINOSAUR bone today!"

He excitedly tells me all about it during our twenty minute call.

He hops off and Miranda's face fills the screen. Sometimes it takes my breath away to see how much Luke resembles her.

"Hey, E. Still getting along out there?"

She still has a soft spot for me I think. We've remained friends through the divorce and has bizarre as it is, we still connect as friends and are quite amicable. I think our shared child- Luke- has everything to do with it. The other part is, she is now happier with her new husband than she ever was with me.

"Yea... All is good."

She smiles at me, "Any time frame on your retirement plans?"

We had talked last time about how after this deployment I am retiring and moving back to the states. This is my last tour of duty. At thirty-five I am tired, ready for the next thing. Time with Luke. Maybe find a woman to settle down with. Unbidden an image of Ryan pops into my brain.

"By that smile, I'd say retirement plans are in full swing."

I didn't realize I'd made any smile.

"Paperwork is in process. This is my last tour of duty."

"I'm so glad. Nobody deserves more happiness then you, Eric."

"Can you do me a favor, Miranda?"

"Of course."

"Can you begin looking at properties there in Pensacola? I want to be close to Luke and you."

Her smile is soft and fills the screen.

"Of course! Luke'll be so happy. What did you have in mind? A condo? House?"

I clear my throat. "House, I think."

"You'll be so happy, Eric. And Luke is going to be over the moon to have you so close. You know he hero worships you."

"Well, that might change."

"Doubtful."

"Well, I've gotta run- I'll email you any potential places I find."

We discussed time frames a bit more then I sign off.

I still have ten minutes online time, so I decide to browse some stateside news. In amid presidential debate articles and football stats for week 2, there she is - Ryan.

The headline reads, SEAHAWKS QB DATING PLAYBOY CENTERFOLD.

Beneath, a picture of them exiting a nightclub together.

My gut clenches. I hover over the link in turmoil. No denying it, I had been holding a torch for Ryan since that NIGHT. In the picture, she's wearing a miniskirt and leather jacket; Her hair still blonde. I'm starting to dislike this blonde version of my fierce Ryan. Her legs are fucking ten miles high and I remember what it feels like to have them wrapped around my waist.

I click the damn link to bring up the full article.

Seahawks' quarterback, Alex Devereaux, is under fire for being "distracted" in last week's game. Critics are blaming his new love interest, playboy model and ex-navy enlisted, E. Ryan. The two have been spotted at Flame, Seattle's newest five-star restaurant, and downtown nightclub, The Penthouse.

That was it.

I considered doing another search for more information. Closed my laptop instead -ignoring the burn in my gut. Did you really think you'd get the girl this time, Broussard?

I guess I hadn't admitted defeat yet.

Butter's comes into the comm room. "Yo! Chief!"

I gave him a grunt back.

"Who pissed in your cheerios?"

I turn to him fully, contemplating. He and Ryan got along and might still be in contact.

"You ever hear from Ryan, Butters?"

"Every now and then, why? What's up?"

Reluctant to share anything with him, I just give a shrug.

"Nothing really, just saw where she was dating some NFL dude."

He gives a half smirk at me, "Oh yea, Devereaux. We aren't known to giggle over gossip and wine, but she did tell me she is in Seattle for a bit."

"Huh."

"You want me to pass her a note in study class, Chief?"

"Shut the fuck up, Butters."

I slam out the door, not giving him any more ammunition.

37

Ryan

Time with Devereaux is relaxing in that I don't have to do a lot of guessing about what he is thinking- he just comes out and says it; A nice change from the last man I was interested in. I've gone to calling him "the last man" in my head as a way to try to expunge all these feelings from my heart.

Our Fall themed breakfast, turned into dinner and a PR appearance. Since I was already in town for the weekend, I stayed for his Sunday game, watching from the VIP booth making small talk with a few of the other player's wives. It felt forced though. Like I was just a puppet making all the right small talk with them when deep down I felt no connection. Their lives seem to be all roses and Coach bags. My life has been bullets and Kevlar. After the game, Alex takes me to another diner for an epic post-game breakfast, but my heart isn't in it.

"Listen, Ryan. I like you a lot." He says while pouring syrup over his pecan waffle. He sets the syrup container down and smiles affectionately at me. Damn.

I've managed not to really read anything deep into these few days, just kinda floating from one thing to another, observing but not really feeling. It has been a joy just to turn off the question of "what's next?" And now, when I feel something-the wrong thing I think to myself-he wants to complicate things.

"I like you too, Devereaux," I choke around my waffle bite.

"So, I gotta know – would you want to continue to date me? See where this takes us?"

I nearly spit up the coffee I just took a sip of.

Before I can form a reply- my phone dings with an incoming message.
I don't look at it. I just pick up my fork and look Devereaux in the eyes.

"Alex," I began, "I'm not good enough for you." I smile to soften the blow.

He looks perplexed.

"What do you mean?"

"It's just that…" I sigh and look out the diner window.

"Since I've been back, I'm not whole. I'm just a shell. I don't think I can be the star quarterback's girlfriend."

I put my hands up in defeat. I hate admitting that. I hate where this whole conversation is going- down the shitter.

Alex is looking intently at me, but I can hardly stand to look back at him.

"It's ok, Ryan. You are the most courageous woman I know, and I think that's why I am willing to wait till your ready."

I smile at his compliment. But hate that he's still got the wrong idea.

"Don't wait on me, Alex." I tell him. "Don't wait to live your life to the fullest. To reach out there and grab love where you can find it. Don't ever wait…Cause life is so fucking short, and…"

I want to go on, but I get a little choked up thinking about T-Rex and David, My mom's face even swims into my vision for a minute, how short their lives were.

Shit. I push half my waffle back and forth on my plate not really looking at it.

I put down my fork no longer hungry.

Looking out into the downtown Seattle night, the people bustling about.

"Come on, Ryan. Let's get out of here."

He pushes out of the booth and drops some money on the table. He puts his arm around my shoulders as we walk to his car. It's nice, but I'm too torn up inside and can't form any words to reassure him that I'm ok.

He takes me back to the hotel and leaves the car running when he comes around to open the door for me.

We both know I'm flying back to San Diego tomorrow. He engulfs me in a hug and doesn't let go.

I start to shiver. He finally pulls back and rubs my arms up and down.

"I'm not going to say goodbye, cause I know we'll see each other again, Ryan."

I give him a smile, but it's half-hearted now that melancholy has settled over me like a wet blanket.

"Thanks, Devereaux."

He kisses my forehead and I wave to him there from the front of the hotel.

My time out in Seattle provides no better answers on moving on with life. In fact I almost feel worse.

My phone buzzes when I am in the elevator. I absentmindedly pull it from my bag.

A call from a Florida number. This time of night, I feel like it's probably not a spam call. I answer it.

"Hello?"

"Fuckin' A, it is the beautiful, awesome Ryan…Watcha doing?"

It's Reed. And he sounds a little shit-faced. This cheers me up a bit. It is three AM East Coast time.

"I'm being a responsible adult and going to bed? What about you?"

Odd that he wants to chit-chat, but I figure I must be the drunk dial.

"Are you going to bed alone?" He strings out the last word and I hear some hooting in the background.

I ignore his question while I open up the hotel door.

"Who are you with, Reed?"

"Letttts see. There's Meaty and, Hanzo, and who the FUCK are You? Oh! That's Broussard. He's driving. I forgot."

All this is slurred, but my stomach knots up when he says Broussard.

"Ok, what's up Reed?"

Might as well cut to the chase on this call.

"You NeVer AnSweRed my text!"

"Oh... I didn't get a text. What did it say?"

"I was inviting you to my Bachelor party and wedding. You gotta come cause Jess says so, and I say so, and Butters says so, and Meaty says so..."

He giggles.

"Well congratulations, Reed. "

"ahh. Thank you...so you'll be there?"

"Umm. When is it?"

"When is it," he pauses and I can tell he's moved his mouth away from the phone when he says, "Meaty, when is it?"

I hear some mumbling in the background.

"Oh! Yea. It's in three weeks. In FLO-REE-DA."

I laugh at his pronunciation. I miss these guys so much. It punches me in the gut. I suddenly want more then anything to just hang out with them.

"Yea, I might be able to make that. You gonna send me all the info?"

"Jess'll do it, now that I got your number."

Broussard

We had luckily enough shipped back a little early, and we were taking advantage with a little celebratory night out.

We are in the bar doing shots when Reed asks Butters about Ryan.

"You got her number, Butters? I'm going to text her and invite her to the wedding."

"Yea, Yea, let's see."

He's scrolling through his phone, and I nonchalantly take a sip of my drink acting for all the world, like I could give two shits about what they are talking about.

"Yea, girl hooked a brother up! Gotta have her at the wedding," Reed continues.

"And what did Jess say when she found out you didn't know a Louboutin from a Chanel?" Says Meaty.
Reed answers, "Ha! Shows what ya'll know about women, I came clean with her the next date when she asked me about her Gucci or some shit, and she thought it was cute that I asked another woman's advice."

Butters breaks in with, "I don't know shit about designer crap or women, what about you, chief?"

"Nope."

Butters continues the conversation, "You think Ryan'll bring that QB with her?"

Meaty: "Shit man, I don't know! What you think Chief? Besides Reed and T- you probably know her best."

I just grunt into my soda.

"You know, I heard something interesting from Peanut," Butters says.

We are all silent and my gut clenches at the thought of what he is going to say next.

"When Ryan showed up at T's funeral, she was wearing her civvies. Nice ones too, he says- really showed off her figure..."

"And your point?" I bark at him.

179

He looks at me with a mischievous glint in his eye.

"Just that he also noticed the two of you left in the same cab together."

I don't acknowledge the whoops that go around the table, just get up and get the next round.

It's on the way home that they really start ribbing me.

"Imma call her right now…" This from Reed.

I notice he's pulling his cell phone from his pocket and it takes all my willpower not to reach across to the passenger side and knock it out of his hands.

Meaty helps me out though with a protest from the backseat, "Don't fucking DRUNK dial a woman- you pussy!"

"She's not my woman…and I am mildly inebriated." Excepted mildly inebriated comes out like "Midly inabriatated."

He's got the phone up to his ear, and I just grip the steering wheel harder in anticipation.

A hush has fallen over the guys as they strain to hear the conversation.

It's three AM- no way she'll pick up.

She fucking picks up. And I am straining to hear every word of her side of the conversation.

She laughs at Reed's greeting.

Pauses at his question about bed. Doesn't answer. Shit. She's not alone. The sting burns in my gut. I'm so mad I tune out nearly the rest of the conversation she's having with Reed.

"Jess'll do it now that I got your number." Reed finishes.

I don't hear what else she says, but he puts his phone down and turns to me with a sly grin.

"Just call me cupid."

The rest of the guys explode into laughter and I just shake my head.

38

Between starting a new job as a civilian contractor at the Pensacola Air Force Base running top level security initiatives and buying a partially constructed house and working to make it habitable, plus spending as much time as possible with Luke, the next three weeks pass rather quickly for me.

It's Friday night and I'm sitting on the deck of the popular beachside bar, Riptides, with Meaty and Butters waiting for Reed's groom duties to finish up. The rehearsal dinner ended an hour ago, but you'd think the bride knew what we had planned and kept making up things to keep Reed occupied and throw a kink in our plans. Good thing, I'm the best man though. I've taken into account such delays.

I sip my almost empty beer.

Check my phone and look over towards the door, where Reed should be strolling through any minute.

Meaty asks, "So, Broussard, you gonna sell your house once you get it all tuned up?"

Our conversation for the past thirty minutes has been about the construction I have been doing on my new digs.

"I don't know. I could list it for quite a bit, but I'm not sure the market's quite peaked."

"I wouldn't hate retiring here in Pensacola. The beach has some mighty fine views."

I chuckle. I know what views it's referring to, women in bikinis. Just then in walks Reed, with a leggy blonde on his arm.

It takes me a minute to recognize who that leggy blonde is. Ryan.

They saunter over to us.

"Ready to get this party started gentleman?" Reed asks.

"Hell yea!" Meaty and Butters respond, rising from our table and giving Ryan hugs in hello.

I stand and drop some money on the table to pay for our drinks.

Reed points over his shoulder and rubs his palms together, "Car is out front, let's ride, ladies! No offense, Ryan."

She puts her hands out and says, "None taken," with a smile.

My three comrades in arms are practically already to the door, leaving Ryan and I to bring up the rear. Her ass is to die for in a pair of painted on jeans. Her shoulders exposed and tan in a fancy red-colored tank top with a hundred sexy crisscross ties in the back. I'll never understand women's' clothes, but these ties are as sexy as hell.

I catch up with her at the door, she's just as tall as me in her heels. I push past her and hold the door open.

"Hi, Broussard." she smiles at me while stepping through.

"Hi, yourself." I smile back at her.

We pile into the waiting SUV, and I sit next to Ryan. Her top is low cut, and I think god silently for the breasts he gave this woman.

Ryan

Sure, I know Broussard is checking me out. I can feel his eyes on my cleavage. That is the whole point of consulting my sisters for their fashion advice for this little trip. I had decided that I could do with one or two more nights of Broussard in my bed. Or the hotel's bed. So, the fashion advice to catch a man was bachelor party: feisty minx, wedding: fresh innocent. They assured me, no man can resist such a combo.

We stop and pick up Reed's brother, Aiden, with Reed's other two soon-to-be brothers-in-law and head to a scotch and cigars bar at a trendy little place downtown. Reed's brother is the only one to protest my female presence when he climbs in the SUV.

"What the hell? What's this chick doing here?"

Reed slaps his kid brother in the back of the head.

"She's one of my very good friends, and here to help me celebrate my impending doom. So don't be a dick."

"Well, hotness," He turns to me, "You got a name?"

"Yea, kid," I tell him, "It's Ryan."

He gives me a lopsided grin that tells me he has had a pre-party and isn't affected by my "kid" label.

"Alllllright, let's Ride!" Reed whoops.

At the bar, I've started my second glass of scotch and water, and doused a half-smoked cigar out in the ashtray when Reed turns the conversation to me.

"So, Ryan. What have you been up to since the Playboy shoot?"

His kid brother interrupts before I can answer, "Wait, Playboy shoot?"

Meaty chimes in, "Yeah, kid. You're looking at the only SEAL ever to be a centerfold." He points his cigar at me with a wink.

"Ha. It was two pages in the very back, Meaty. I mostly did it to get the CIA recruiters off my back."

Broussard is sitting in one of the club chairs directly across from me, and the look he gives me. It's annoyed disapproval all over again. I just can't seem to ever get it right with this man.

"Well, it was a mighty fine spread," Butters compliments with a raised glass.

I look at Reed and Meaty and we just start laughing at Butter's pun.

Thankfully, the conversation then turns to our next stop, the defining event of all bachelor parties, a strip club.

39

Broussard

I had reserved a booth at Babe's, the strip club. We are sitting back from the stage a bit in a VIP booth, and I am happy enough that Ryan seems relaxed and happy where she is, flanked in the middle of the booth by Meaty on her left and Reed's kid brother on her other side.

Of course, Reed's brother is relentlessly hitting on her, but she seems to ignore it mostly. It is when I get the second round, and occupy Reed with a lap dance that I notice Aiden turned towards Ryan with his mouth up to her ear, his arm along her shoulders.

I flip. Running through my veins is something damn near psychotic jealousy and possessiveness.

I stand up and go around to where Aiden is sitting.

"Hey kid, take a lap dance on me."

I hold out a twenty.

He gives it a questioning look, but gets up.

"Got to take a piss-break anyways." He says to me without taking the twenty.

I just ignore him and plunk down next to Ryan.

She's gone quiet again.

Thankfully, Meaty is there to pick up the slack.

"So Chief, you did a mighty fine job planning this party."

"Well thank-you, Meaty. It sure as hell beat any of my bachelor parties."

"Oh-ho! Bachelor parties?" Ryan questions.

"Yea. Married twice. Can you believe it?"

"With your winning personality? I don't believe it," She scoffs.

"Babe, it's not my personality the women love," I flirt back at her.

She blushes a bit at that and takes a sip of her drink, while I'm transported back to the memory of the first time we met.

We watch as Butters slips some money into the G-string of one of the girls onstage.

"You can always tell the ones that are classically trained," Ryan breaks in.

"Huh? Classically trained?" Questions Meaty.

"Well...guess it takes one to know one." She laughs out.

"What do you mean, 'takes one to know one?'" I ask as an image of Ryan stripping pops into my brain..

She looks at me. Takes a breath in so that her cleavage rises up. I try not to look, but fail.

"I trained to be a ballet dancer before I joined up."

Reed and one of his future brothers-in-law rejoin the group.

"No way," Reed says. "I don't see it."

"Well, you don't have to believe me…" Ryan returns.

"Prove it." Says Meaty.

"Prove it?" She questions.

Reed goes along with this idea. "Yea, give us some fancy twirl-twirl shit."

"All right," she states before climbing over me.

I get a pretty good chubby when she practically sits in my lap. But she's over and out the booth before I can even savor the feeling.

She reaches back to the table and downs a shot. She's looking a bit tipsy, glowing and flushed.

"For...you know courage," She says. She then places her hand on Reed's shoulder for balance and slides her shoes off. Tucks them under the table with her feet.

She points her toe out to the side and then brings it in, the momentum initiating her spin. One full revolution, two, then three on the ball of her foot. Then she stops with a little bobble, not entirely graceful. She bows and a couple of the strippers clap their appreciation.

She sits back down next to me (I have to quickly scoot over or she would have been in my lap again) while pulling her shoes back on and laughing.

"Damn. I'll drink to that!" Meaty says with a grin while raising his glass to his lips.

Reed takes a spot at the table, while one of the professionals starts chatting up Ryan.

"Girl, you need a job?"

Ryan laughs and shakes her head.

"I'll leave it to the real professionals."

Aiden comes back then, leading a professional by the hand.

"I bought you a lap dance, Sugar," He tells Ryan.

He's lucky the use of the name 'Sugar' doesn't land him with permanent brain damage.

"Yea?" Says Ryan very nonchalantly.

"Yea. Even got you a private room. So we can enjoy it together."

Slimy little cocksucker.

"How nice of you…" Ryan says and then turns her head fully to me.

"But, I think you should take the man of the hour, your brother. Besides, Broussard and I were just about to get the next round of drinks."

She pulls me up by my hand and I make sure to wrap my arm around her shoulders as we head to the bar.

"Gawd," She says when we get there, "He just won't take a clue."

I lean up against the bar and take a good look at her.

Her eyes are rimmed in black eyeliner, making them stand out. Her lips are pouty, almost bee-stung and if it wasn't in fashion I'd say they're obscene. A little blush, and her trademark short hair, in blonde with artfully messed up waves.

"Well, Sugar," I put extra emphasis on the sugar, "You're probably the only playboy bunny he's ever gonna meet."

She sighs at that, and yells the drink order over the bar to the bartender.

"Yea."

We gather up the drinks and deliver 'em back to the table.

But she doesn't sit down. Instead she goes up to Reed and gives him a hug, while telling the guys,

"All right assholes. I'm going back to the hotel and catch up on my beauty rest so you can let your...hair down."

Meaty and Butters give her hugs and goodbyes.

Aiden says, "I'll walk you out."

That slippery weasel sure is fast. Good thing I'm older, wiser and have brute strength on my side.

I take Ryan by the arm and tell him, "I'm walking her out, kid."

Ryan

I had had quite a few drinks and feel relaxed. I really do enjoy the guys company, but strip joints really aren't my thing, and I know I am probably crimping their style.

I say my goodbyes to Reed, and assure him I'll see him tomorrow at the wedding. The hugs from the rest of the guys make me feel cared for, and I know I am making the right decision to leave a little early and let them have their fun.

Of course, I am just about to tell Aiden I don't need his help, when Broussard grabs me by the elbow.

He looks as he usually does, annoyed, when he tells Aiden he'll be walking me out.

Had he even broken into a smile tonight?

We get outside the door and into the parking lot when I pull from his grip.

"Jeezus. Broussard, what's your problem?"

"My problem?"

"Yea, you don't have to manhandle me. I may have had a few drinks, and don't usually wear heels...but I can walk, ya know?"

I pull my phone from my purse and start to bring up a car ride app.

"Joe can give you a ride back to the hotel and come back for us."

He's steering me over to the rented SUV that was hired to drive us around tonight.

"Oh. No worries. I can catch a ride with Uber." I hold my phone up so he understands.

"Just get in the car, Ryan."

"Sheesh. Ok."

I go around to the passenger side of the black SUV while Joe (who has rolled down the window at our approach) and Broussard converse.

"Joe, can you take her to her hotel and then come back and pick us up?"

"Sure thing, Chief."

I roll my eyes as I buckle in.

When I look up Broussard is at my window, so I roll it down.

His visage has transformed from annoyed to concerned and I feel myself melting at the handsomeness of his face.

"You need a ride to the wedding tomorrow?"

The wedding is on the beach at sunset, the reception following across the street at a old hotel from the 1950's.

"Um. I don't think so." Gah. I sound so lame. Speak with confidence, Ryan.

"I'll pick you up. You can help me with my best man duties and all that. Seventeen thirty. Be ready."

I just nod and thankfully, Joe puts the vehicle into gear sparing me anymore awkwardness.

We roll out of the parking lot and I have something new to worry about - my 'date' with Broussard tomorrow.

40

Broussard

Am I making the right moves with Ryan? I'm not sure. But I know I want to convince her to stay a while in Pensacola. I want to show her everything I've done with the house. I checked with Reed to make sure she didn't have a date before I asked her. He assured me she only RSVP'd for one.

If I am honest, I wanted her to see the house because I had done it all with her in mind. Her cooking in the kitchen, her standing on the deck with a glass of wine in her bikini, her in the bedroom with nothing on, I'd pictured it all while installing appliances and countertops, laying floor, finishing out the deck, and painting the bedroom.

I mull over possible conversation topics while I pull to a stop in front of her hotel. She is already standing, waiting for me in the hotel entrance way.

She fairly takes my breath away with her classic grace. Wide leg white pants, linen is what I think they call them, a sliver of tanned skin playing peekaboo at her midriff and a sleeveless top in a black print that shows off her cleavage. A sleek and simple gold necklace drapes against the tanned skin of her breasts..

"You look beautiful." I tell her simply.

"Thank you. You do too. Well look handsome," she finishes.

I give her my arm and escort her to the passenger side of my new truck.

"Where's the jeep?"

"I sold it," I tell her, "terrible gas mileage."

I get in the driver's seat and we continue our conversation.

She laughs, "Does this tank get better?"

"A bit. But I really needed something to haul building supplies in."

"Ah, yes. Reed told me you had been renovating a house on the beach."

"Not renovating. Finishing is more like. The contractor went bankrupt before they could put in all the finishing touches. It was just a shell, really. Walls, windows...not much else."

"And, where did you learn to do all this...finishing?" she asks me.

"My dad is a house contractor. Most summers of my high school years, I spent with him laying tile or putting up sheetrock. And, what I didn't know, I Googled."

She laughs at that.

I am damn near giddy from the whole conversation we are having. Of course, Ryan being Ryan, once I have the truck in park, she is already out before I have the chance to come around and open the door for her.

When I step up next to her and offer her my arm again, I notice our faces aren't level. Her face is level with my shoulder.

"No heels tonight?" I ask while looking down at her feet, her toes are peeking out.

"Nope. Too much trouble between sand and dancing."

I nod my agreement, and tell her, "You can either hang out here at the hotel bar till it's wedding time, or you can come across to the beach with me and watch us all take pictures."

"Hmm. I'll go to the beach," She says, "as long as you don't think I'll be in the way."

"Never," I tell her.

Ryan

I love the beach. And to see it with a wedding, it's so romantic and beautiful that I am irrationally jealous of Jessica, Reed's bride. I find a place away from the chairs and decorated arbor/alter, on a little mound of sand and take a seat.

Pulling off my flip flops, I bury my toes in the sand and listen to the ocean.

This part of the beach has just a few people milling about besides the groom's side of the wedding party and photographer.

I close my eyes and feel the warmth from the sun on my face and shoulders.

I could live here, I think. Just me, the ocean, and the sun.

I open my eyes and watch the photographer position Reed, Broussard, and Aiden in front of the altar. They look good and my appreciation for Jessica's taste goes up a notch.

Instead of having Reed and Broussard wear their dress uniforms, she's got all three in cream colored suits, white linen shirts, casually unbuttoned, no ties with white flowers pinned to their jacket lapels.

Broussard even has on brown leather flip-flops. His feet, of course, as sexy as the rest of him.

I watch as the photographer positions them this way and that. Snapping group shots in various poses, while Reed's and Broussard's impatience grows, I can tell by looks on their faces. The photographer must sense it too, as soon they are dismissed and the first few guests started trickling across the road to the beach for the ceremony.

Broussard scans the beach and stops when his eyes come to me. I stand up and brush the sand from my butt.

He beckons to me, and I walk over to where he was standing just off to the side of the altar with Aiden.

"Just twenty minutes to go, and we've got official duties," he says to me, "Bride or Groom side?"

"Groom," I tell him and let him escort me to a middle row.

Meaty appears in the aisle, and after greeting Broussard with a handshake and man-hug, tells me, "Scoot down one more Ryan, Butter's is gonna want to sit with us."

Broussard leaves to escort guests and family to their seats then and before I know it, we are standing as the bride walks barefoot in the sand to her groom.

During the vows, I can't help but feel my eyes get dewy. Not because weddings are heart melting and sweet, but because I am thinking about moments such as these that T should have been here for. Thinking of T then has me thinking about David, and wondering for all the world if things had gone as we had planned what type of wedding we would've had. The words spoken are simple and direct, with prayers and blessings for the new couple. I squash down my melancholy and harden my heart.

My eyes slide to Broussard standing next to Reed, and I can't help but be pulled into his magnetic gaze.

"Do you, Noah John Reed, take Jessica Elise St. Clair, to be your lawfully wedded wife?"

"I do."

"And do you, Jessica Elise St. Clair, take Noah John Reed to be your lawfully wedded husband?

"I do."

"You may kiss the bride."

Cheers and whoops erupt, and I stand pulling my gaze from Broussard's. My cheeks feel warm.

41

It is a great reception. I dance with Broussard, eat some cake. I stand up and pretend I want to catch the bouquet- but leave it to one of the bride's sisters to catch. I shake the feeling that I shouldn't be here, and surrender to the moments.

Soon, we were directed by Reed's mother-in-law to gather sparklers from a basket and head out to the parking lot for the send off.

I can feel a pounding at my temples.

I slip through the doors while everyone is occupied lining up, and head to the beach. The moon is shining brightly, nearly full and I can see the wet sand glistening in the light.

There are a few kids with flashlights running around looking for crabs, but I can hardly hear them over the crashing sounds of the surf.

I am lost in my thoughts, my memories.

My feet lead me along the beach, and back to the high-rises condos that are the newest construction of the beach. I pause and look up at their artificial lights, and realize I just walked five miles without saying goodbye to anyone.

I pick out the condo I am staying in and keep walking the six hundred or so feet to its wood decking.

Once I get up to my room, I kick off my flip flops and do my own flop onto the bed.

I dig my cell phone out of my pocket and see I have two missed calls and four text messages.

I realize it was probably rude of me to just leave without a word. But, it was that or stick it out with an awkward goodbye to the guys later in the night. With the potential of tears.

Something like panic squelches out of my stomach when I think about Meaty, Butters and Reed all going back to fight.

And leaving before being confronted with the reality is my way of taking back control.

I text Broussard back, *Walked back to the condo. Thanks for the ride.*

It sends and I pull up Google, searching for hair salons close by.

It's time to take back something else of mine too.

Broussard

I watch Ryan's tall form cross the street and stand on the beach for ten minutes after the send-off.

From the way she is standing, contemplating the ocean, I know that this is a time she'd probably like her space. Heaven knows I have been in that same exact posture a million times myself, that same mood, of being lost to the memories and resenting anyone that pulls you out.

She is leaving, I can feel it in my bones; but maybe I can at least finish out the night with her before the forever goodbye.

I go back to the open bar, deciding to let her come back to the party in her own time. The wedding dancing is continuing on, and I grab myself a beer and sit down with Meaty and Butters to wait her out.

Our conversation turns reminiscent as they are always want to do when the members of the team get together. And, before I know it I am at the bottom of my beer, swilling back the last lukewarm dregs.

I pull out my phone and text Ryan.

Gave it five minutes before getting up and walking down to the beach.

There is no sign of her, and the beach is fairly deserted.

I call. No answer.

I go back to my truck and consider possibilities. She is a grown woman. A SEAL. No reason to worry.

I have to fight the instinct to jump in the truck and drive up and down the beach. Instead I try calling again. And when I get no answer this time, I give up and go in to tell Meaty and Butters goodbye.

Back in the truck, I send one more text in hopes that she'd at least let me know she has gotten back to her room safe and sound.

42

Ryan

I have a flight out Monday morning. A full day in
Florida's paradise to do what I want, and I used that
morning to get a massage and am now meeting up with
Butters and Meaty for a late Brunch; afterwards I have a
hair appointment to go back to as close to my natural hue
as possible. It just feels like time to shed the blonde
bombshell. She didn't have answers anymore than I did.

I sip on a mimosa while waiting for the guys to show
up.

They'd probably laugh their asses off at seeing me
drink such a girly drink, but the restaurant has a special for
a nine dollar bottomless glass and I am feeling relaxed
enough to indulge.

They greet me with the usual hugs and happy smiles.

We order and get down to what we do best, giving
each other shit.

"So Reed's handed in his man-card, who's next?" I ask
them.

Meaty leans back in his chair and gives me a skeptical
look.

"Shit girl, we thought it'd be you. How can we get season tickets. I ain't no Seahawks fan, but I wouldn't mind scoring some tickets when they play the Texans."

"You know that was over before it started, Meaty." I tell them.

"Huh," He responds.

"So no tickets?" Butters interjects in the silence.

I throw up my hands, "You two are impossible."

Our breakfast arrives then and the conversation turns to their return to base, catching up on the latest gossip with the rest of the team.

The bill comes, and the guys and I wrap up our conversation.

"So, Ryan, you just heading back to Cali? Got any plans?"

I smile at Butters, and knock back the last little bit of my mimosa.

"No plans. I'm as free as a bird."

"Maybe you should go check out Broussard's beach house."

I push my chair back from the table and give him a hug.

"You're sweet, Butters."

It's only once I'm done at the hair salon that I check my phone- Butters has sent me an address. And I don't need twenty guesses to know whose address it is.

I pay for my new color, cut and style. Back to honey brown with blonde highlights and short and spiky.

It's close to four in the afternoon, and I catch a Uber back to the condo.

Thinking about Broussard. Wonder what he's doing. Before I can analyze my actions, or talk myself out of it, I order another Uber.

I'll just do a drive by. See what his house is all about. I tell myself.

Only when I get in the Uber and we drive twenty-five minutes down the highway, and the high-rise condos disappear, I'm irrationally homesick.

can't figure out this feeling. The sun is dipping low, there are dark clouds building above us. I unroll the window and let the salty sea air hit my face.
Intake the scent.

WHAT DO YOU WANT?!?!! I scream to myself in my head.

There is an echoing silence. *I don't know...* seems to be the only answer.

The driver stops at a concrete mammoth of a house, and I take a look down the road and notice all the houses seem to be set a good distance apart, their long drives denoting an aura of wealth.

Just as I hand the driver a ten from the back seat the heavens open up in a torrential downpour.

I dash along the drive, thank God Broussard doesn't have a gate yet, and up the stone steps to the front door.

I take a heaving breath and ring the doorbell. Seconds tick by, where I brush the raindrops from my forehead to prevent them from running into my eyes.

The door opens.

"Jeez, Ryan! Get in here!"

He pulls me into the foyer without even a question as to what I am doing there.

He is gone, and in the sudden silence and coolness of air conditioning I shiver.

He is back, towel in hand, which he wraps around my shoulders. He begins rubbing my arms up and down with his open palms in an effort to warm me up.

It brings our faces within inches of each other.

I am drinking him in. His strong jaw, piercing hazel eyes, coral pink lips set in a disapproving line.

"What are you doing here?" He asks me.

His hands still on the outside of my arms.

"I don't know." I tell him.

He smiles a bit at that- just one corner of his mouth turning up.

He leans toward me and warm lips meet my own. I close my eyes and savor his tongue against my own in a slow caress.

My hands reach up between us, his warmth, his clean masculine scent is heady and enveloping me.

This isn't what I came here for.

I push at his chest while taking a step back to break the kiss.

My brain registers the house I'm in -cataloging details, in an effort to push away the feelings that kiss erupted in my chest.

It's a large space, the back wall comprised entirely of windows. I can only make out a deck through the windows, the rain is falling so heavily a gray curtain obscures any beach views. Directly in front of me, a step-down to what I suppose will one day be a living room- but right now sits empty, it's concrete floors shiny, yet warm. To the right, is a solid wall, in which the center is nestled a fireplace. To the right of the fireplace stairs lead up to a short loft-style hallway. Doors closed.

To the left, the most beautiful kitchen I've ever seen in my life. Enormous kitchen island, bar stools beckoning for me to have a seat. Gleaming stainless steel appliances, granite countertops, warm cabinets. It makes me wish that I knew more than how to sauté up some chicken breasts. Above it, a loft area.

"Here Ryan," Broussard grabs my hand and leads me over to the kitchen.

Behind the back wall of the kitchen is a staircase up to the loft, and just beyond that, a tucked away laundry room.

Broussard pulls me into it, and pulls some clothes from the dryer.

"Still warm," he turns to me handing me a dark gray t-shirt and pair of black boxer shorts.

I instinctively take them from his outstretched hands. "Thank you."

"You can change in here," he's putting the other clothes from the dryer into a laundry basket on the floor, "And then put your own in the dryer."

I nod my ok, and his warm body brushes against mine as he leaves the room.

I take a deep breath and the warm scents of homely cleanliness soothe my wildly beating heart.

I peel my cold, wet jeans down my legs and throw them in the dryer. Bring his t-shirt up to my face and inhale. Tide detergent and something else. Something masculine. Something uniquely Broussard.

I pull my shirt off and over my head, and throw it into the dryer after my jeans.

My bra is damp, so I hang it up on one of the convenient rods placed along the back side of the wall.

The towel and my underwear both go into the dryer before I pull the warm t-shirt over my head and his shorts up my legs.

I leave the laundry room and find Broussard in the kitchen, leaning into the refrigerator.

He stands up when he senses me enter the kitchen. In his hand a bottle of wine.

"My Ex left this here when I moved in...I don't know if it's any good..."

I look at the label. Chardonnay.

"Just a glass." I tell him.

He uncorks the bottle and pours into a nice wine glass.

"I'm afraid she still thinks she can refine me, hence the wine and glasses."

I take a sip, while leaning my hip against the island countertop.

"It's nice." I tell him.

He reaches back into the refrigerator, and I admire his lats and shoulders this time.

He comes out with some craft beer bottle in his hand.

"Or, if you want you can try this IPA."

He cracks open the top with a bottle opener that was within easy reach on the countertop.

Takes a sip.

My eyes drink in his form. Tight gray shirt pulled taut over his chest and shoulders, khaki colored shorts worn and comfortable.

I reach forward and snag the bottle from his fingertips. Take a sip myself. It tastes bitter after the sweet, cool wine.

I purse my lips and hand it back to him. Outside, a wind gust lashes rain against the windows.

"I'll stick with the wine. Compliments to your ex."

He lifts his beer bottle in a toast, and I return with a lift and tip of my own wine glass.

"I'm grilling steaks as soon as this rain passes over, you want to stay for dinner?"

He says it casually, as I am studying the granite pattern of the countertop.

Broussard

Please say yes, please say yes.

"Umm. Yes. That sounds nice." She says.

She's tilting her head to the side, studying me, but I'm doing the same to her. Her long, lean and tan legs are sinfully on display in my boxer shorts. Her breasts are swaying freely underneath my t-shirt. It's all I can do not to go over there and run my hands up under her shirt with glee at having her braless in my kitchen.

I clear my throat and turn back to the refrigerator in an effort to hide my growing erection.

"You like a good 'ole romaine and ranch salad?" I ask her as I pull ingredients from the refrigerator.

"Yea, that's good…" Her voice is drifting away.

"What's the story on this house, anyways?" She's peering out the back windows, the rain has died down to just a steady sprinkle, and the white sand beach and gray-blue ocean are visible now.

"Oh. The developer that started building it went bust. He paid primo for the concrete, hurricane grade windows…but couldn't finish it out. So it was just a shell when I bought it. Just needs it's finishing touches."

"Hmm. nice deal then?"

"Yep. My ex-father-in-law owns a local construction materials company- so I was able to get a lot of things at discounted prices…the tile for the bathroom, these cabinets and granite countertop…"

I'm not really sure she is listening to me though, her eyes and entire focus seem to be on the ocean out the window.

I tell her, "Why don't you go on out? I'll be out in a minute to fire up the grill."

I put the sliced romaine into a big bowl. The rain is barely a sprinkle now.

Putting the steaks on a plate, I season them.

A feeling of contentment washes over me as I take the steaks, my tongs and beer out onto the deck.

Ryan is facing out towards the sea, her wine glass sitting by her hand on the railing. Her feet are crossed at an angle, and the wind is causing her hair to flutter lightly in the wind, the strands still damp. The storm clouds are lifting at the horizon where the sun is setting, giving us golds and grays in the sky.

This is life. Everything I really want right here. Good food, good woman, it's home.

I fire up the grill, and walk to stand next to Ryan while it heats up.

Her scent is tantalizing, like grapefruit and coconuts.

I reach up and catch a strand of her hair.

"Back to the brown?" I ask.

It's probably the least of my smoothest lines, but sometimes I am just adrift at sea when I am around Ryan. My usual pick-up game is non-existent. My usual flippancy towards women- gone. It doesn't take a genius to know that it's because I'm damn near in love with her that makes me all sixes and sevens.

"Blonde bombshell wasn't really me," is all she says in response.

"Well, I much prefer the real you. This you." I tell her.

"Broussard," She looks at me.

"Eric." I tell her.

"Eric," she says, "What are we doing here?" A pause and a sigh. "What am I doing here?"

She looks away from me and down into her wineglass like she expects to find the answers there.

I grab her hand and raise it to my lips.

"Just enjoying a glass of wine, a nice view, and hopefully a delicious dinner." I tell her.

Her beautiful cool gray eyes are measuring me, contemplating the truth in my words.

She tugs her hand out of my own and uses it to raise her wine glass to her lips, taking a sip while returning her gaze back to the sea.

"You have a beautiful house, with a beautiful view."

"I do." I say without looking away from her.

She turns to look at me, noting that I am looking directly at her when I state my agreement.

"I'll be right back, gotta put the steaks on."

What passes in the next hour is a comfortable relaxed dinner in the company of an extraordinarily beautiful woman.

43

Ryan

After finishing my steak and salad, I grab Broussard's plate and my own to carry inside. I place them both in the sink and began washing them.

"Hey, you don't have to do that."

I turn to find Broussard has followed me in, carrying my wine glass and his beer bottle. This side of him is so different from the military man I know.

"I know. I just...thanks for the steaks, they were good." I tell him while rubbing my hands dry on a hand towel he has hanging from a drawer.

"Would you like one more drink?" He says from behind me, "We can lounge under the stars and watch the moon rise over the water."

"I really shouldn't..." But he already has the wine pulled from the fridge and is filling up my glass.

"That's just sensibility talking," he says, "let's live in the moment."

His words ring in my ears- echoing a ghost.

"Sounds like we are surrendering to the moment..." I tell him. I walk out onto the deck and select one of his loungers to lean back on.

He follows and lays back on his own lounger and we listen to the waves and watch the fading twilight.

I'm transported to another beach, another weekend, with another man.

The sun is high, the wind rolling off the Pacific caressing my bikini clad body. David reclines on the blanket next to me, Ray Bans on, Boston Red Sox hat flipped backwards on his head, beer in his hand.

He reaches past me and into the cooler to get a new can. Dropping ice cubes in my lap along the way.

I screech and fling them off me.

"Very nice, David."

"You looked hot, babe."

I look over at him, his abs and chest glistening with sweat in the sunlight. He pops the top and takes a deep pull from his beer.

I think I love him.

Sure it's been just a year since we met, and most of that time it's been crazy weekends at his apartment that he rents with two other guys, or the occasional weeknight he'll show up at my dorm...But, I just love this guy.

I smile at him, "We should get Shcmick's for dinner tonight."

He rolls his eyes at me, "You always want the fancy stuff, Everly.....is'nt Phil's just as good?"

I laugh at him. "If your diet is as restricted as mine, cheat days are the days you have to go for the good stuff."

"Well, I guess I can treat my girl, just this once..."

It was at that dinner he told me he was being deployed. A tear escapes the corner of my eye and I dash it away with the back of my hand.

Sheesh, maudlin after two glasses of wine, I guess there is a lot of truth to alcohol being a depressant. I look over to see if Broussard's noticed, and sure enough he's looking at me with concern in his eyes.

"I should probably go." I say.

"You can talk to me you know, Ryan. I make a good shoulder to cry on."

I sigh, cringe at laying myself out there, ripping out my past hurts for someone as strong as Broussard.

"I'm just overly tired...it's been a long weekend..." I pause and take the last sip from my glass and sit it on the deck, "Hell, it's been a long ten months." I finish.

And to my embarrassment, the truth in that statement has more tears leaking out of my eyes.

I throw my arm above my head in an effort to hide them from Broussard.

I hear him stand up, and before I realize what he's doing, he has his arms slid behind my back and under my knees and is lifting me up against his chest.

"C'mon, Ryan. Bedtime."

I'm sniffling, my eyes bleary in effort of holding back unshed tears as he carries me up the staircase behind the kitchen into a loft space. There is a platform bed, unmade with the fluffiest looking comforter I've ever seen in my life. The bed is pushed back against the wall, underneath skylights. Again the wall facing the ocean is floor to ceiling windows. Broussard places me down on the bed and pulls the blanket out from underneath my feet.

"Here. Just relax. Rest. I'll be right back."

The bed's cool sheets, the blanket warm above me, maybe just Broussard's presence moving around the house is all affecting me like a tranquilizer. My eyes are heavy and I close them.

44

I wake in confusion. I stumble from the bed, taking note of the glorious sea vista splayed out in front of the windows. I shake my head, remembering that I am at Broussard's house and look behind me for a place I can relieve my urgent bladder needs. There's just one door, and I open it to a white marbled space, with a superlative tiled shower and gleaming white countertops. I take care of business, and splash water on my face. My stomach rumbles, so I head down the stairs and into the kitchen.

It's only then that I register the voices. Not a voice. But two distinct voices. I walk the short hallway and enter the kitchen.

Broussard is there at the stove, cargo shorts, t-shirt, bare feet and spatula in hand.

At the table, a mini-person, a boy with blonde hair sits while coloring quietly and humming.

I look down at what I am wearing. My nipples are standing at attention, pushing against the soft fabric of Broussard's t-shirt in an obscene manner. I grab the material at my stomach and pull it outwards.

I look up, hoping nobody has noticed my entrance.

Only they both have.

"Luke, I'd like you to meet Ryan. The lady I told you about before."

I smile at the small human at the table.

"Ryan, this is Luke, my son." Broussard states proudly while indicating the small human at the table.

He's looking at me expectantly, in fact they are both looking at me with twin expressions of expectancy.

"Um. Hi." I give a little wave.

This seems to pass approval, because Luke goes back to coloring while Broussard gives me a kiss on the cheek. "You look beautiful." He whispers at my ear before returning to the stove.

Once there he commands, "Sit down, Ryan. We're having pancakes."

"Um. Ok." I sit.

My brain cells don't really function in the morning. Or at least, they take a good cup of coffee and twenty minutes to kick into gear.

"There's a boy in my class named Ryan," the little human says to me.

"Yea?" I return in my ever-loquacious morning-speak.

"He says dinosaurs are stupid and wipes boogers on his desk."

"Ugh...that's terrible?" It comes out as a question.

Thankfully, Luke is adept at carrying on conversations, and picks right up without noticing my hesitation.

"Everyone knows dinosaurs are awesome!"

He lifts his paper up to show me a half-colored dinosaur.

I nod and Broussard places a cup of coffee into my hands.

I take a deep sniff of the brew and feel my synapses start firing.

"Do you have any cream or sugar?" I ask Broussard.

"I got milk...Will that work?" I nod yes, while he places it on the table by my hand.

I pour some in my cup and take a sip.

"What do you get when you cross a dinosaur and a firecracker?" I ask Luke.

"What?"

"Dyno-mite."

Broussard's chuckles. Luke giggles.

"What kind of Dinosaur is a cop?" Luke asks me.

"Hmm. I don't know, what kind?"

"A tricera-cops!"

We laugh at his joke. Broussard sets a pile of pancakes down in the center of the table and we dig in.

"Do you know anymore, Ms. Ryan?"

"Oh. You can just call me Ryan... I think that's the only dinosaur joke I have."

Luke finishes his pancakes and jumps down from his seat.

He places his finished picture under the only refrigerator magnet and says, "Dad, can Ryan come fly the kite and build sand castles with us today?"

Broussard looks at me, "Well, Luke, that's entirely up to Ryan."

They both look at me again with mirrored expressions.

"Oh. Uh. I actually have to get back to the condo and pick up my stuff. I have a flight out later this afternoon." I tell them.

Luke breaks the silence first with, "That's sad. We are gonna get a dinosaur kite, aren't we Dad?"

"Yep. A dinosaur kite. Go get dressed and get your shoes on so we can go and pick it up."

Luke races across the empty living room and up the stairs to one of the far bedrooms.

I stand up and put my coffee cup in the sink.

I turn back to where Broussard is still seated at the table.

"I'm sorry I didn't tell you earlier," he says. And we both know he is referring to the fact that he didn't tell me he had a kid.

212

I shrug and tell him, "It's ok."

He runs a hand through his hair. "No, no it's not. I want to have a relationship with you, Ryan. And that starts with being open."

I didn't really hear anything after his "I want to have a relationship with you, Ryan." My heart beat has accelerated, butterflies in my stomach.

"...A relationship? With me?" I ask him.

"Well yes. I thought..." He stands and looks out the window, "...I thought that was what you wanted also."

His jaw muscle is clenched, his arms crossed in front of his chest.

Is a relationship what I want? I'm flummoxed.

"Honestly, Broussard...I'm not sure what's possible between us. I didn't really analyze my actions in coming here..."

I trail off hoping the truth will soothe his temper.

He turns from the window and runs a hand through his hair while looking down at the floor.

"What reason could you possibly have for going home to California now? I see you Ryan. I see a hurting depressed woman. You're fucking lost and not going to admit it."

I'm speechless at his words. Nobody has been so brutally honest with me before.

He grabs me by the back of the arms.

"You've lost weight, you've got bags beneath your eyes, and dramatically changing hairstyles left and right. Don't think I don't know too, that you're skipping out on the required rehab -both physical and mental."

I pull away from him. Annoyed and weirdly pleased he's concerned about me.

"Jesus Fuck. Who are you? And who the fuck have you been talking to?"

His eyes are studying me, his face a mask of flat fury. His words hurt, but he doesn't stop.

"You want to go home and be some NFL dude's wife? That's fine. Fucking perfect. Go live that life. But I know you Ryan…"

He stops abruptly. Closes his eyes on a sigh. "Just hang out with us, with me, a few days. I know you love the beach. It'll be chill. No worries."

There's hope in his voice, and I find that the thought of hanging out with him, doing silly things like building sand castles and lying about the beach does sound appealing.

And he's right about Devereaux. That isn't my life, which is why I gave him up those three weeks ago.

There's just one tiny human blocking me from giving in.

"What about Luke?" I ask him.

His face relaxes a bit in question, but it doesn't ease the nerves circling in my chest.

"It's just kids…" I wave my hand in the air trying to explain the overwhelming panic that sets in when I'm around them.

He must sense my anxiety and pulls my hand into his own, while bringing his arm up behind me to pull me against his chest in a hug.

"It'll be fine, Luke's great. You'll see." He says into the air above my head.

45

That afternoon found me sated from the best picnic lunch and relaxed under an umbrella, watching Broussard explain the finer points of flying a T-Rex kite to Luke. I ignored the irony that he picked a T-Rex kite. I was committed to doing what Broussard had said, chilling. Plus I just feel too exhausted to fight anything anymore, Broussard included. It is just easier to lay on the beach towel, under the shade he had so proudly made for us by erecting the sun umbrella.

Or is this happiness? Content in Broussard's presence because his capability and responsibility make it so I can just follow his orders like a good soldier.

I am not sure the reasoning, but something inside my chest has loosened. The weight of sadness I've been carrying from the one-two punch of forced retirement and T's death seems to lighten just a little.

Broussard hands off the kite to Luke, who immediately takes off running.

I smile a bit at his exuberance.

Broussard plops down on the beach towel next to mine, but keeps his eyes trained on his son.

"That little turd just wears me out. Or, I'm getting old." he laughs out.

It's refreshing to see him smiling and happy, even though I didn't put it there, it lifts the sad weight a bit more. Or it could be hormones reacting to his stupid handsome face. I'm not sure.

"Tell me about him, Broussard. How'd you get him?"

He laughs at that. "The old-fashioned way, Ryan."

I blush a bit.

He laughs some more and says, "God Ryan, how can you still blush after all the shit you've seen?"

"Ugh...Just tell me about Luke." I say to change the subject.

"Well, it's not a long story. My first marriage didn't last the length of my first deployment. Typical story-married after high school, I went to basic, she went to college. On my first deployment she couldn't stand the loneliness and cheated. So, the second time around I made sure to pick a good one."

He pauses and my heart jumps with jealousy. Seems he still has a fondness for her.

"Miranda is a nurse. Works in the ER, I met her through a bar pickup...We dated two years and got married. Everything was good. Well, as good as a marriage can be during multiple deployments. And when I was home, she wanted to start a family. And I agreed. While we were trying and amid deployments we just realized that we were better friends than lovers. Or hell, maybe it was the stress, or the loneliness but I think Miranda just decided she didn't want to be a soldier's wife anymore. I can't fault her. She gave it to me truthfully. She sent me divorce papers along with Luke's pre-school pictures."

"Shit," is all I can think to say.

He gives a half grin at my response, but doesn't take his eyes off Luke running back towards us.

"Yea, it fucked up my head a bit."

We are quiet for a moment, the spell broken only when Luke comes up to us.

"Dad. Tie up the kite so we can build the sandcastle."

They may have done this before, because soon Broussard has the kite sailing merrily behind us, having staked the lead string into the ground while Luke digs in the sand.

He starts up a conversation with me. He is the most eloquent six year old I've ever met.

"You like sand castles, Ms. Ryan? First we build the moat."

He demonstrates for me, finishing with, "... then the walls, then the circle building."

"The tower," Broussard fills in for him, coming back with a bucket of seawater for the building of the castle.

Broussard shapes sand with his hands and says, "Tell me about the C.I.A. Ryan. How that led to the playboy shoot."

I watch him square up a wall.

"It's not a terribly long story." I tell him.

"I'm listening."

We both watch Luke take the bucket to the surf.

When I got home, it started simple enough. Calls, letters, emails asking to set up interviews — that sort of thing."

He nods his head.

"Seems easy enough to avoid."

I agree with him. "...Those things are easy enough to ignore. But the personal visits. And the damn near stalking when I went out. Those were annoying as shit."

Luke is carrying an bucket of water back to us, his body leaning to one side as he struggles with the weight.

Broussard doesn't get up to help, but just tells him, "Good job, buddy," When he gets close enough.

They mix a bit of the water with sand in another pail to form a second tower.

"I'm still listening." Broussard starts the conversation back up.

217

"Uh-huh, well. I just decided it was time to take back some control. Get the monkey off my back so-to-speak. And if there is one thing the CIA finds undesirable, it's notoriety."

Broussard

I watch Ryan fill a bucket with a sand and water mixture and tip it over to make a corner of the castle.

For the most part she is quiet, just listening to Luke talk.

I slap myself mentally for feeling contentment at the picture they make together- a mother and son happily playing in the sand. That's not the reality, Broussard. Pull your head out of your ass. She may only be here a few days.

Which is why exactly I need to savor this moment. Go all in.

I playfully tap Ryan on the ass when she gets up to get another bucket of seawater.

"Tag, you're it." I tell her.

She narrows her eyes at me and drops the bucket, casually walking back to Luke who is watching us.

She taps him on the head and sprints backwards yelling, "Now you're it!" to Luke.

He grins and runs after her.

She circles back around to me, and Luke sets his eyes on a new target, maybe easier he thinks, as I am just laying in the sand. I let him tag me.

Then I lazily stand up, eyeing my target. She's standing just ten feet away, merriment in her eyes, poised to run.

I start, and she takes off. I catch her before too long, and throw her over my shoulder. Luke who has followed us in excitement bounces along in the sand.

"What should we do with this troublemaker, Luke?" I ask him.

He laughs at us but comes up with a suitable punishment.

"Throw her in the water!"

"No! No!" she laughingly yells from her perch on my shoulder. She is half-heartedly struggling now.

Luke starts running circles around me as I trek to the surf.

I get thigh deep and drop her in.

She comes up laughing and sputtering and splashing me and Luke both.

It's a beautiful sight.

46

Ryan

"Pew! Pew! Lieutenant Luke, get agent evil!"

I fire my nerf gun from behind the corner wall at the standing action figure of "Agent Evil."

I'm deliberately missing so Luke, standing at the opposite corner wall can shoot him down with his own nerf gun.

We are on maybe the third set of this. I grab the extra nerf gun I have at my side, and when Luke runs out of ammo, I slide it on the floor down to him.

"I'll get him, Captain Ryan!" he shouts at me, coming out from his position to get closer to the action figure.

Just then, the doorbell rings and it's such a strange sound to my ears. The mundaneness of it breaking into our action packed afternoon drama.

Eric comes in from the deck and says to Luke, "That'll be your mom, Luke. Do you need help gathering up your stuff?"

Eric is halfway to the door now, and I am broken out of my stillness- sliding the storm trooper helmet off my head.

"Awww Dad. Can we kill Agent Evil one more time?"

He laughs, shakes his head no, and looks to me for backup.

I start picking up the spent nerf ammo, just as Eric pulls open the door.

"Miranda, so good to see you, come in."

I stand up and take in the wildly and hugely pregnant woman that steps into the foyer.

She smiles at me and steps down into the living room, arms outstretched.
"You must be Ryan."

She engulfs me in a hug- her perfume cloud light and sweet. I helplessly look over her shoulder at Eric.

He's got a half bewildered, half happy look on his face.

Her belly is huge between us, rigid and weird.

Eric shrugs his shoulders as if to say, "I don't know, just go with it."

"That's me. Ryan," I tell her while patting her shoulder.

She finally pulls away and must see the look on my face, "Oh! I'm sorry. It's just that Eric has told me so much about you. And I just get carried away sometimes these days."

She waves her hand in the air as if to dismiss any awkwardness and turns back to Eric asking, "Babe, can I use your bathroom? I have to pee."
Eric doesn't even blink at her term of endearment, instead ushering her into the downstairs guest bathroom, a hand on her back.

She comes back out, a whirl of happy, glowing motherliness in a floral dress. Uneasiness settles in my gut as I watch her and Eric from the doorway as he loads Luke in the back of her car, giving him one more hug.

Luke waves to me from the backseat as Eric shuts Miranda's door for her.

I feel disenchanted. Detached from the scene in front of me. The love of this family shine out from their eyes. I am a stranger in their midst.

Broussard

Seeing Miranda off, I'm sure I couldn't have asked for a better ex.
She tells me from where she is sitting in the driver's seat, "Oops. I'm sorry Eric, I think I scared Ryan a bit."

She fiddles with air conditioner vent, pointing it directly at her face so it blows her hair off her shoulder.

"Nah," I tell her, "it's fine. Ryan's just...Ryan." I shrug my shoulder.

"Stupid man," she chuckles, "I hope she sticks around, seems like she's a good fit for you."

She puts the car in gear and backs out of the drive.

I give her and Luke one last wave.

I climb the steps to the front door contemplating the ways I might be able to seduce Ryan into bed. The past few days has been all about innocent fun, chilling on the beach, the torture of seeing her laying about in her bikini, keeping me in a state of near arousal.

The chill air of the air conditioning beats back the humidity as I step inside. Hard to believe it's October. It's damn near silent as a tomb. I always get the same immediate feeling of missing Luke whenever he leaves. I chop it up to the sound level dropping twenty decibels.

I don't see Ryan on the deck, in the kitchen or living room, so the most obvious place she can be is upstairs in the bedroom. I climb the back loft steps, and hear the shuffling of her moving about.

She's got her bag on the bed, and is throwing clothes in. My stomach drops at the same time I become immediately pissed off. Why is she leaving?

"What the fuck, Ryan?"

She folds a pair of jeans and places them on top of her bag.

Looks up at me, and I can't read what's behind her gray eyes.

"Eric," she starts, "I'm going back to California."

"No you're not." I state flat out.

"Why? What's here for me? Huh?"

She picks up another shirt and folds it.

"ME!" I yell at her, then realize my anger is the direct result of my fear of losing her, seeing her slip through my fingers...I drop my voice and calmly tell her, "I'm here for you."

She looks at me, sadness in her eyes. Sits down on the edge of the bed and puts her head in her hands.

I cross over and kneel in front of her. Taking her hands away from her face, I'm near shocked by the tears in her eyes.

"Stop punishing yourself for their deaths, Everly. You are not to blame. I'm not to blame. It's shit luck, and bad guys. But our time to live is here. We owe it to them to live the best life we can. It's what they fought and died for. It's what we fought for."

She pulls her hands out of mine.

"What do you know about it, Huh? Your life...It's so fucking easy for you. You have..."

She trails off without completing her sentence and falls back on the bed, once again throwing her arms over her face.

Ryan

I feel his hands warm on the outside of my knees. It's a steady comfort when my emotions are in turmoil. The grief, guilt, anger are all swirling in my throat ready to explode out.

SHERRY L. BROWN

His hands move up along my outer hip, up in a slow caress which he follows with his body.

Once above me, he uncrosses my arms away from my face and kisses my eyelids, forehead, cheeks...covering my entire face in soft caresses.

A delicious slow burn begins deep in my core. He's moved on to my neck and upper chest. He pauses to peel my tank top up and over my head. I pull his t-shirt over his own head in reciprocation. The view of his muscled chest, defined abs, and ridges along his lats turns me up another notch.

Without hesitation his warm chest is against mine, his arms around me as we kiss deeply. Tongues entwined in a dance while his body, his center presses oh so good right where I need.

He breaks away, only to slide down to my hips, and kneel on the floor between my legs.

He traces his tongue just above and along the waistband of my jeans. It tickles and arouses me at the same time.

He pauses when his tongue reaches the center button. Exhales heat against my vulnerable belly.

Undoes the button, and slowly drags the zipper down.

Only when his hands dip into the waistband at my sides does he look up.

I understand his want and lift my hips to aid in the release of my legs from the denim.

I'm wearing my serviceable black hip hugger underwear. Sure it's silky-soft to the touch but hardly bombshell material. He drops his head to my pubic bone and inhales.

"Babe, you're driving me crazy," he breathes against my center. The vibrations and heat of his words go straight to my clit and I feel the moisture slick at my entrance.

He rubs his nose against the fabric, while his hands smooth up the inside of my thighs.

He tugs my panties down and off my legs.

For seconds I am laid bare for him, and the tiniest niggle of insecurity slithers in my mind. He is looking down at me, and unreadable expression in his eyes. He leans down and kisses first, one inside hollow of my leg, where the lips meet the thigh, then the other. His repeats the movement, this time changing the kiss so his tongue gives a caress.

The sight of his bent head between my legs coupled with these soft passionate kisses is my devastation.

I close my eyes and sink into the sensations, as he continues to lavish tongue kisses and caresses on my outer lips, then inner lips, and even dipping down to do a broad stroke against my entrance. I'm torn. I want him to use his wicked tongue on my most sensitive button, but loving all the other attention. Suddenly his arms grip the outside of my thighs and he pulls me closer to him. The back of my legs are now pressed against his shoulders. His forearms on the outside of my thighs. I peek my eyes open and see his return gaze just as his right hand reaches the skin right at my pubic bone and pulls - exposing my clitoris- he dips his tongue down to taste it and the sensation is heaven.

He's licking in broad flat strokes from my entrance to my most hot button. I grip the sheets and enjoy the strokes, but in my mind's eye I'm picturing his magnificent cock, the hot steel velvet in my hands, against the folds of my pussy.

"Eric," I breathe out, "please."

He speaks against my core.

"What do you want baby?"

"You." I tell him.

He stands up and drops his pants. He's breathing just as hard as I am. And holy mother of all that is holy. This is what I've been waiting for. His cock, unabashedly, brazenly erect, free for all my pleasure.

I sit up and cup his balls with one hand, while the other circles his thick phallus.

My fingertips don't meet. I bring my lips to the head. Feel the satin heat with them. Close my eyes and dart my tongue out to dip in the opening there. Swirl my tongue around the head. Delicious heat.

Smile at Eric's intake of breath. Look up to meet his eyes.

"Jesus, Ryan," he groans and pulls away from me.

I lay back and he follows me down. The head of his dick is poised at my entrance.

He grabs the sides of my head in his hands.

"Say you'll stay, Ryan."

I close my eyes, and thrust my hips up in an effort to get him to enter me.

"Say it, Ryan."

I grunt in frustration. I grab his butt with both my hands, taut muscles in my hand. I attempt to pull him down, while I thrust up.

"Just stay and I'll give you what you want." He smooths the hair on the sides of my head.

I open my eyes and read the need in his.

"Fine," I agree.

He thrusts home and the sensation has me spiraling to new heights. I lose myself in every heavenly thrust of his hips, whimper when the scorching heat of his dick leaves my body.

The pressure builds and builds, until the explosion leaves my insides quivering and my mind blank.

47

I listen to his heartbeat, feel the rise and fall of his breath. He's relaxed. I'm relaxed in a weird wrung out way myself. I find that words are choking in my throat- threatening to erupt in an undignified spewing. I want to talk to Broussard. Make him understand.

"I was supposed to have the American dream. Married. Kids. Minivan, soccer games, white picket fence, golden retriever."

He doesn't say anything to my statement. Just rubs a hand down my back and sweeps it up again. His fingertips dance over the scar on my shoulder.

"But," I continue, "I knew after I hadn't been able to Skype with David for three weeks that the worst had happened. He'd been K.I.A."

I take a deep breath in and hold back on the tears threatening to squeeze out.

Eric kisses my forehead and gives me a squeeze.

"Sshh. Baby. You don't have to tell me this now."

"No..." I tell him, "I want to. I need to."

"I didn't make his funeral. His mom and dad, they didn't know we were engaged. They just thought...I don't know- that I was a casual fling?"

He continues to rub my scar with his fingertips.

"After school was out, I took a flight out to Boston, I met his parents, went to his gravesite. My sisters said I had to do it for closure."

He squeezes me in a bit closer to his chest.

"When I was there, looking down at this tombstone- I just got mad. Mad at the whole fucking world for this stupid fucked up shit we were in. And mad that David had to die for it. I couldn't understand. Hell, I still don't. So, I made him a promise. I promised that I would do everything in my power to protect the men that were still over there- so that no other woman- girlfriend, fiancée, wife, sister, daughter – would ever have to feel this way. I vowed I'd never feel this way again- useless, you know? You think that's stupid?"

Broussard is quiet a moment.

"No, I don't think it's stupid. I think it's courageous."

"Well, you might be the only one. My entire family thought I went off the deep end when I packed up my dorm room and enlisted that summer."

"But your dad, he supported you right?"

"Not until I left the Marines. I think he realized I was going to do this with or without his help, so he took it upon himself to get the higher ups to admit me into BUD/S. I'm sure he thought I'd ring out sometime."

We are both quiet at that- he knows my history from there.

"What about your mother?" He suddenly asks.

"Hmph. My mother. That's another can of worms for different time." I tell him.

"Don't close up on my now, Everly Ryan."

I sigh and roll to my back. He follows and props his head up on his elbow.

"You don't think her death had anything to do with the path you took?" He asks me.

Did it? She had me so late in life, I think back to how fast she declined once she found out she had breast cancer.

"She died when I was seventeen." I tell him, "I think I was pretty well set in my ways by then."

"Bullshit. You choose a path that put you on the road to becoming a ballet performer. Your college was centered around dance."

"Yea, it was. It was ingrained in me. I'd done it since I was three. Hard to figure out what's habit and what's enjoyment when you do something that long."

"But you gave all that up, no issue, Everly. Don't you see?"

"No…" I tell him.

"You told me once in the desert that you weren't made to sit at home and bake cookies. Well, you weren't meant to be the frou-frou ballet dancer either."

His words comfort me in a strange way. Like he might be the only one in the world that sees me for who I am, even when I am blind to myself. I lean up and give him a kiss on the cheek.

"I'm going to jump in the shower." I tell him.

48

I wake up again disorientated. The sun is streaming down on the bed from the sky lights. I roll to my side and inspect the nightstand looking for my phone. There is a note folded on top of it.

I sit up in the bed and unfold the paper.

Ryan, I had to go to work. Make yourself at home. I'll be home around 4. - Eric

I am not concerned. There's definitely a bit of relief in my belly that we don't have to hash out our "relationship" this morning after a night of incredible sex and over-sharing.

I step into his amazing bathroom and strip down while the water in the shower heats up.

I let the hot water massage my neck and shoulders while I contemplate. I'm no closer to answers than I was three weeks ago. I know I like spending time with Broussard. I like the beach. He's retired now, so it's not like I have to worry about him being deployed again. On the other hand, he can be totally invasive, domineering and just plain frustrating. Those qualities also translate well to a complete master in the bedroom. So what if I stay here as long as he'll let me? The only fear holding me back from saying yes is the commitment of a new relationship. Is this what I want?

I picture Broussard at the kitchen sink washing dishes, or folding my clothes after they come out of the dryer. Gawd, yes I want this easy domestication. I want to wake up in a warm, soft bed and feel a man's heat behind me. Get up and enjoy lazy Sunday's watching football and drinking wine. Having phenomenal shower sex, and not having to worry about dodging bullets or patching up friends.

I turn off the shower and grab a towel. I notice my moisturizer on the counter next to Broussard's beard trimmer. Looks like I've already claimed half his space anyways. I take my toothbrush out of my travel bag and place it in the cup next to Broussard's. There. That wasn't so hard.

I spend the morning doing another load of laundry. I only had a few outfits with me, thinking I'd only be visiting for four or so days, so supplementing my wardrobe with t-shirts from the Eric J. Broussard collection has been essential. The short time in between doing laundry loads is becoming tedious.

I send a text to my sister after putting the clothes in the dryer.

I need a favor. Can you head over to the pool house and grab some of my clothes. Whatever you can fit in a 2-day shipping box. Please? I watch the three little ellipses as she types back.

Instead of a text though, my phone vibrates and her contact picture comes up with an incoming call notification.

"Hey, Kinsey."

"OH MY GAAWD. EVERLY RYAN. Are you shacking up with Broussard?" She screeches over the line.

"Um, yes?" It comes out as a question, I thought she'd be happy for me- and I can't quite read what her tone is over the line- motherly concern or excited sister.

"I can't believe it. Independent spinster is ready to throw in her title for a little military man meat action."

I huff indignantly at her, but don't have a comeback. Is that how she saw me, spinster? I mean I get that I am twenty-eight and have only had one boyfriend, but spinster seems a little harsh.

"Will you send me my clothes or not?"

She laughs.

"Of course I will, just wait till I tell Iz."

A sudden clatter sounds in the background.

She says, "Oh shit! I got to go Everly. Text me the address."

Before I can even say ok, the phone hangs up on her screeching to her kid. Sheesh. Domesticated life I'm ready for, motherhood I am NOT.

49

Broussard and I have settled into an exciting and pleasurable coexistence. He skipped work on Tuesday afternoon to take me to a car dealership at my request. Laughed when I specified that I wanted a Jeep. But dipping into my savings account and paying for a barely used wrangler in gleaming white made me almost as happy as foreplay with Broussard.

When I followed Broussard home in it, he opened the garage door and insisted I park it inside, so I didn't have to worry about putting the top back on. There I discovered he had been holding out on me- he had a 70lb punching bag hanging from the ceiling in the second garage bay. I'd be back tomorrow to give it a good workout.

On Wednesday, I was high off a night of great sex and fresh from a sweaty punching bag session when I decided I should take my new jeep for a jaunt to the grocery store to buy ingredients to make Broussard a thanks-for-the-orgasms dinner.

But once I got to the fancy grocery store close to his house, I realized I don't really know how to cook. I dialed Izzy from the parking lot, looking for some cooking advice. "Oh my gosh, so the rumors are true," she says when I tell her why I am calling.

"Look Iz, can you help me out or not?"

"Yea, yea. What skill level are we talking here?"

I groan, "It's bad. Protein shakes and salads."

I'm not above throwing myself on her mercy. She is the only person I know that bakes regularly and I'm pretty sure her husband and kids aren't surviving on toast and water.

"Ok. We're going Italian. You can't mess this up, because you are going to buy the sauce that's in a jar."

"I like where you are going with this," I tell her. She finishes up her instructions, and I hastily jot down the ingredients on the back of a gas receipt.

"Thanks Iz. I owe you."

"Well, to be honest Everly, I am just so happy you've called me more than you ever have before. You may be five hundred miles away in Florida, but I feel closer to you now than I ever did when you were off doing god-knows-what in only god-knows-where."

I cringe a bit, the guilt hitting me full force.

"Yea, Izzy. It's good to call," is all I can think to say of in reply.

We disconnect, and I gird my loins for this foray into domestication- the grocery trip.

50

I punch the bag every morning and sweat out the desperate anxiety of the uncontrollable. Then I run along the beach. I remember. Force myself to relive happy memories. Normal things. Non-combat things. Like how my mother used to do my hair in braids and buns before ballet class. How David used to sneak into and out of my dorm room. How T-Rex and I used to laugh over lifting weights and terrible cafeteria food. I remember the normal. And then I dive into the ocean and let my tears be washed away by the sea. Every day for a week. And at night I feel the lust, heat and passion that is new love. We conversate over dinner, sometimes he cooks, sometimes I do, and sometimes we get takeout. We walk along the beach, or watch a movie in bed. Just enjoy normal couple things.

I'm not blind to what's going on. I'm healing emotionally, spiritually. But while it hurts deep in my soul, I feel the catharsis is needed. More than that, I embrace it. It's a Thursday afternoon. A cold front has finally come through, and I sit on Broussard's deck in his oversize fleece pullover and yoga pants. I'm skimming through colleges, researching places where I can get a physical therapy degree, making to-do notes on my new laptop. Physical therapy popped into my brain after my run this morning, and it felt right.

The sound of the doorbell ringing drifts out the open door to me.

I place my laptop on the kitchen counter as I go in to answer it.

"Miranda. Hi."

Her face is pinched, and Luke clings to her hand with a worried expression on his own face.

"Ryan. Is Eric home? I tried his cell but he's not answering."

"Uh, no, he's got a couple hours left at work. Can I help? Do you want to come in?"

She places her hand on her belly and sucks in her cheeks while closing her eyes.

My own widen. Shit. I hope this isn't an active labor situation.

"Yes, you can help," she continues with a slightly alarmed face, "I need you to drive me to the hospital, and stay with Luke."

My brain stops. She's trusting me to take her to the hospital? And watch her kid?

"Uhhh. Ok. Just let me grab my shoes and keys."

She bends over and reaches her hand out, I instinctively give her my own, which she squeezes painfully.

"Just hurry; we'll take my car," she says while turning back towards the driveway.

I don't waste any time. Just close the back door, slip Broussard's flip flops onto my feet (they are the closest shoes), grab my phone and wallet and head out the door behind Miranda.

She's already got Luke strapped in and sits in the passenger seat.

The SUV is still running when I take the driver's seat.

I put the car in reverse and ask where we are going.

"Uh-oooowwww. University hospital. My water broke just twenty minutes before I picked Luke up from school. I thought I'd have enough time to get him here and get checked into the hospital before the contractions got close together…"

She does some complicated breathing thing as we pull up to a stop light.

I look in the rearview mirror at Luke. He's sitting quietly with a worried expression on his face.

"Everything ok, Luke?" I ask him.

"Yea, Ms. Ryan. I just…is mom going to be all right?"

Miranda answers before I have a chance to.

"Yes, honey. I'll be fine. This is just part of the process."

She gives me a roll of her eyes.

I pull into the turn for the hospital and park at the emergency entrance. I'll come back and move the SUV once pop-any-minute-Miranda is in a doctor's care.

I thought these crazy give-birth-any-minute type situations were just T.V. and movie drama. What do I know? I pull Luke from the back seat and carry him on my hip. He's a bit big, but I can manage. Miranda's already at the doors, and they whoosh open for her.

"We need a wheelchair here!" I yell as I walk towards the admitting desk. "She's got contractions, water broke, what forty-five minutes ago?"

Miranda nods her agreement. The admitting nurse stays studying her paperwork, not even glancing my way.

"How far apart are the contractions?" she asks.

"Six and half minutes," Miranda answers.

This spurs some action on the admitting nurse's side. She speaks into a radio mike clipped to her shirt. Fires another round of questions at Miranda, who answers them succinctly and still calm.

A wheel chair is brought for her, and she whisked up to general delivery.

I follow behind with Luke still in my arms.

Watch as she is placed in room, hooked up to monitors, and signs paperwork.

"Where's your husband, Miranda? Shouldn't he be here?"

"OH!" she hisses out on a breath. I watch the contraction monitor needle bounce up and sustain for several moments.

"Yes, ROB IS SUPPOSED TO BE HERE. BUT HE"S AT A CONFERENCE IN MIAMI."

I pull my phone from my back pocket and dial Broussard.
I am the least qualified person to be with Miranda in a time like this.

He doesn't answer.

I text. Take Luke into the hallway when they do the down there check.

When the nurse comes back out, she says to me,

"Mrs. Broomfield is in active labor, and will be delivering soon. You'll need to take her son here and wait in the waiting room. I'll have the doctor come get you when the baby's delivered and you can see her."

Luke tugs on my hand.

"Ryan, can I say bye to my mom before we have to go?"

I look at the nurse. She smiles at him.

"Of course. She'd like that."

I lead Luke back to Miranda's bedside. Her hair is plastered to her forehead, and a nurse is beside her hooking up an IV.

Luke climbs onto the bed beside her and gives her a hug. She holds him for a minute.

The motherly picture crumbles a piece of my stone heart.

"Ryan. I'm sorry I didn't really even ask."

"It's ok," I tell her.

"Rob's on his way here, he's should be here in about three hours. He's just texted me that he's got a flight."

"Sure, no problem, we'll just be down the hall in the waiting room."

She nods and gives one last kiss to Luke's forehead.

He waves to her from the doorway.

Broussard

Labor and delivery. Never thought I'd be here again. Ryan and Luke are napping together on the little couch in front of the T.V. in the waiting room. It's sweet. I don't wake them up just yet, instead I check in at the nurses station. Get Miranda's room number. I'm just going to pop in and let her know I've got Luke for the weekend and that everything's all right. The sight of her holding her newborn daughter gives me pause. Tugs at my heart. Miranda looked hopeful when she turned to the door, but her smile drops just a bit when she sees it is me.

"Oh. Eric. I thought you might be Rob."

"He'll be here soon?" I ask her.

She nods and says, "Yes, any minute actually. My mom too."

I cross over to get a better look at the new baby. Pink blankets swaddled tight around a wrinkly tiny face.

"She's cute, Miranda. Good job."

Miranda smiles and says, "Thanks Eric."

"I've got our own kiddo to take care of, so I'll leave you to it."

"Make sure you give Ryan a big hug for me, Eric. I just commandeered her help. She did good. Don't let that go."

As I come back out I take a moment to savor the picture Ryan and Luke make on the waiting room couch - Ryan's wild tousled locks and Luke's small form tucked into her side. I notice that curiously, Ryan is wearing flip-flops two-sizes too big, and my fleece pullover. Satisfaction and caveman like happiness roll through my heart.

I gently shake them awake.

"You two hungry?" I ask.

"Are we leaving dad? Do I get to stay at your place?"

"Yea buddy." I answer him.

Ryan is standing, but looks confused. I grab her hand in my own while Luke runs over to the elevator and pushes the button.

"Can we go through the drive-through, dad? Please?" he says.

"Oh I don't know…" I say even though that had been exactly my plan.

He jumps up and down in the elevator. Supercharged-after-nap Luke.

I sling my arm around Ryan's shoulder as we walk through the parking lot. Ryan doesn't get supercharged after naps, I can tell she's still groggy.

"So, how about some salty French fries and a cheeseburger?" I ask her.

She runs a hand down her face and looks at me.

A smile tips up her lips.

"Sounds good."

As the hospital doors whoosh open for us, I instinctively look for Luke's hand before we enter the parking lot. But the little imp is already on Ryan's right side, holding her hand as we step away from the curb.

ABOUT THE AUTHOR

Two years ago Sherry had an epiphany. Life is what you make it- and she was ready to make it HERS. So, she grabbed the bull by the horns and quit her job at a tech startup to pursue personal passions and adventure dreams. She successfully taught herself graphic design. She hiked 558 miles through southern California on the Pacific Crest Trail. And she wrote this book. She'll keep courageously jumping full force into life regardless of the success or failure of her dreams, with her husband of ten years and her morkie, Petey, by her side.